Ghost Stories
of an Antiquary

I

A Graphic Collection of Short Stories by M.R. James
Adapted by Leah Moore and John Reppion

SELF MADE HERO

First published in the UK 2016
by SelfMadeHero
139-141 Pancras Road
London NW1 1UN
www.selfmadehero.com

Introduction copyright © 2016 by Ramsey Campbell

Publishing Director: Emma Hayley
Sales & Marketing Manager: Sam Humphrey
Publishing Assistant: Guillaume Rater
UK Publicist: Paul Smith
US Publicist: Maya Bradford
Designer: Txabi Jones
Editor: Dan Lockwood
Cover by: Francesco Francavilla

A CIP record for this book is available from the British Library

ISBN: 978-1-910593-18-9

10 9 8 7 6 5 4 3 2 1

Printed and bound in Slovenia

PICTURES THAT LIVE

M.R. James (1862–1936) refined the tale of supernatural terror and, given his fondness for narrative play and overt references to generic tropes, can be cited as one of the field's first modernists. His ghost stories are a British institution. I've seen them praised for their cosiness, their atmosphere of academia and Edwardian male camaraderie, and their reputation for providing a comfortable shiver or two. I would say all this underrates and misrepresents the author's contribution to the genre. Far from being cosy, his stories frequently present a reassuringly ordinary setting that is invaded by the malevolent and terrible. Sometimes everyday objects take on or harbour hideous life, and at times the juxtaposition of these elements borders on surrealism. He was among the first to make the tale of supernatural terror as frightening as possible, an effect he achieves by an inspired and precise selection of language. Many of his most effective moments are inseparable from his style. No writer better demonstrates how, at its best, the ghost story or supernatural horror story (either term fits his work) achieves its effects through the eloquence and skill of its prose style – and, I think, no writer in the field has shown greater willingness to convey dread. He can convey more spectral terror in a single glancing phrase than most authors manage in a paragraph or a book. He is still the undisputed master of the phrase or sentence that shows just enough to suggest far worse. Often these moments are embedded within paragraphs, the better to take the reader unawares; the structure of the prose and its appearance on the page contribute to the power of his work. If you know his tales, think about this: how many of them can be conjured up by remembering just a few words – "of crumpled linen", "a lungless laugh", "a mouth, with teeth", "filled and sealed", "and *put its arms round my neck*"? They're a great memorial to his commitment to horror with reticence – in his essay **Ghosts – Treat Them Gently!** he cites both as essential elements – and proof of his posthumous power. His influence remains crucial to the field.

Given that his effects depend so strongly on the selection of language and the timing of his prose, we might wonder if it would be redundant to illustrate his work. He didn't think so himself. His first collection, **Ghost Stories of an Antiquary**, was illustrated at his behest by his friend James McBryde, who drew four images but died before he could complete his version of Count Magnus (unless, as some sources have it, the piece went missing after his death). Since then there have been many visual bids to conjure up his spectres, and now the talented team of Leah Moore and John Reppion have transformed the first four tales from that first book into graphic narratives.

Let me say at once how many Jamesian qualities they preserve. Their selection of the original prose is judicious, and as much of James's dialogue as possible is used, though some invention is unavoidable (and, I think, very much in the spirit of the author). Like James, their adaptations take time to establish the setting and a sense of history, that element that persistently and in general malevolently invades the present in his stories. Indeed, the pacing of these adaptations is authentically Jamesian. Moore and Reppion are adept at conveying the gradual accumulation of unease his work depends upon, as the minor characters in particular betray fears they can't quite conceal and knowledge they might prefer to keep to themselves (see not just their expressions but their fearful postures too). When the horrors are revealed, they're both true to their literary source and powerfully reimagined: see, for instance, Aneke's depiction of the demon in Alberic's book, as much like a spider in human form as one could wish (or perhaps wish not) to encounter. "Lost Hearts" has been visualised before, as one of Lawrence Gordon Clark's ghostly Christmas treats on BBC television, but the Moore-Reppion treatment is quite as effective and affecting, from its overwhelmingly avuncular Abney to the interplay between Stephen and the servants – all the suggestive subtleties of dialogue and behaviour are here. Nor does it stint on terror, and the two nocturnal scenes glow with the light of nightmares, rendered visible by Kit Buss.

In a sense "The Mezzotint" is ideal material for graphic adaptation, since its central issue is a kind of comic strip – an engraving invaded by a ghostly intruder, which goes about its ghastly business but is never observed in motion, thus transforming the mezzotint into the equivalent of a series of frames in a strip. Might James have had such a resemblance in mind when conceiving the tale, or was he perhaps thinking of the motion picture? Moore and Reppion summon up a sense of cosy academia, and Fouad Mezher's images impart an elegiac quality, not least in the nostalgic use of colour (which is expressive in all four of the stories here). His pictures come to life, rather as the engraving does in the tale.

"The Ash-tree" is a strikingly bleak version of one of James's bleaker works. It begins in English legend – the witch who turns into a hare – and ends by mustering far more monstrous manifestations. While several of the author's tales make us look at pictures that are ominous or worse, some of which we've seen here, this story takes the voyeuristic notion further and makes us spectators at a scene where there are no human witnesses, the horrid death of Sir Richard Fell. Where the original tale shows this purely through simile and indirection, Alisdair Wood lets us glimpse the nature of the creatures that share Sir Richard's bed. I fancy they are as grisly as their creator would have wished.

And what might he have made of this latest incarnation of his work? He wasn't always too gracious about accepting tributes. Adrian Ross dedicated a fine supernatural novel – **The Hole of the Pit** – to him, and I assume James must have seen it, but there's no record of any response. When he was sent a copy of **Supernatural Horror in Literature**, in which H.P. Lovecraft enthused at length about his work, he simply scoffed at Lovecraft's prose. Nevertheless I'm going to presume he might have liked the celebration of his work within our pages here, and I certainly think it's worthy of his memory. Otherwise, who knows? Perhaps that cold draught at the back of my neck is more than that, and the object that has landed on my shoulder to claw at it isn't merely a dead leaf enlivened by a breeze, particularly since it seems to be gaining substance. Once I've rounded off this introduction and sent it to the publishers I shall have to turn and look.

Ramsey Campbell
Wallasey, Merseyside
18 May 2016

CONTENTS

All stories adapted by Leah Moore and John Reppion

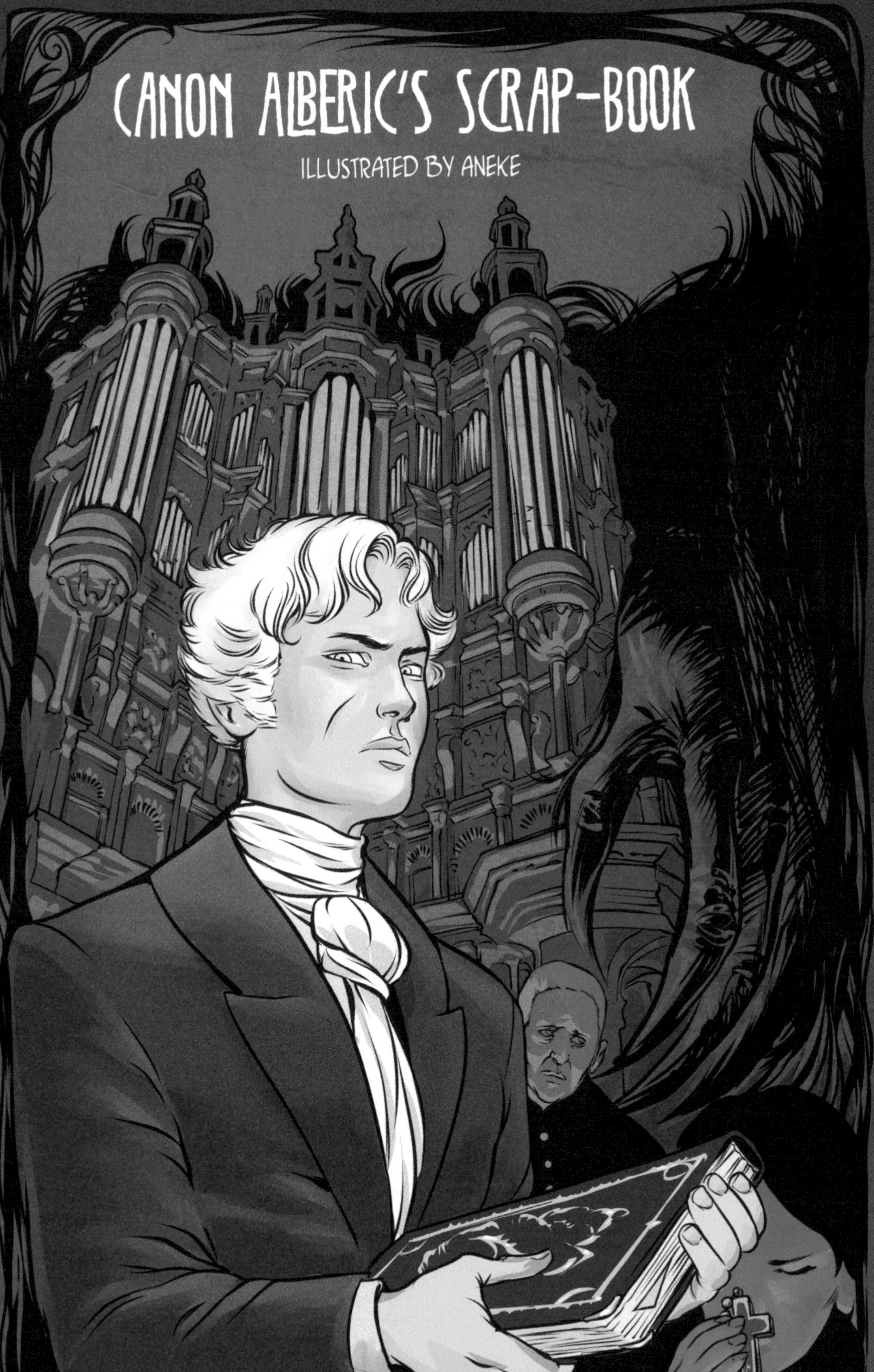
CANON ALBERIC'S SCRAP-BOOK
ILLUSTRATED BY ANEKE

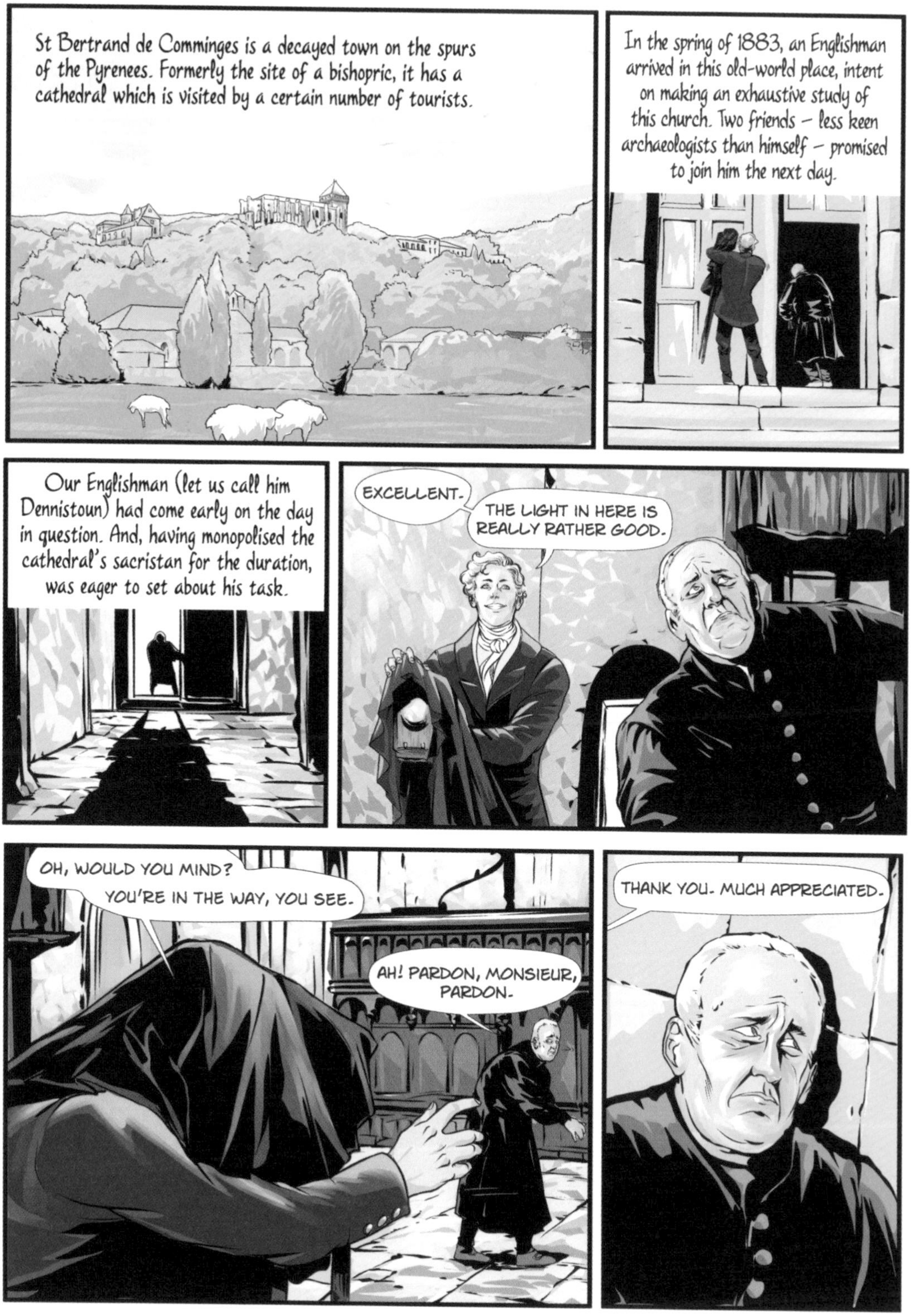
St Bertrand de Comminges is a decayed town on the spurs of the Pyrenees. Formerly the site of a bishopric, it has a cathedral which is visited by a certain number of tourists.
In the spring of 1883, an Englishman arrived in this old-world place, intent on making an exhaustive study of this church. Two friends – less keen archaeologists than himself – promised to join him the next day.
Our Englishman (let us call him Dennistoun) had come early on the day in question. And, having monopolised the cathedral's sacristan for the duration, was eager to set about his task.
EXCELLENT.
THE LIGHT IN HERE IS REALLY RATHER GOOD.
OH, WOULD YOU MIND?
YOU'RE IN THE WAY, YOU SEE.
AH! PARDON, MONSIEUR, PARDON.
THANK YOU. MUCH APPRECIATED.

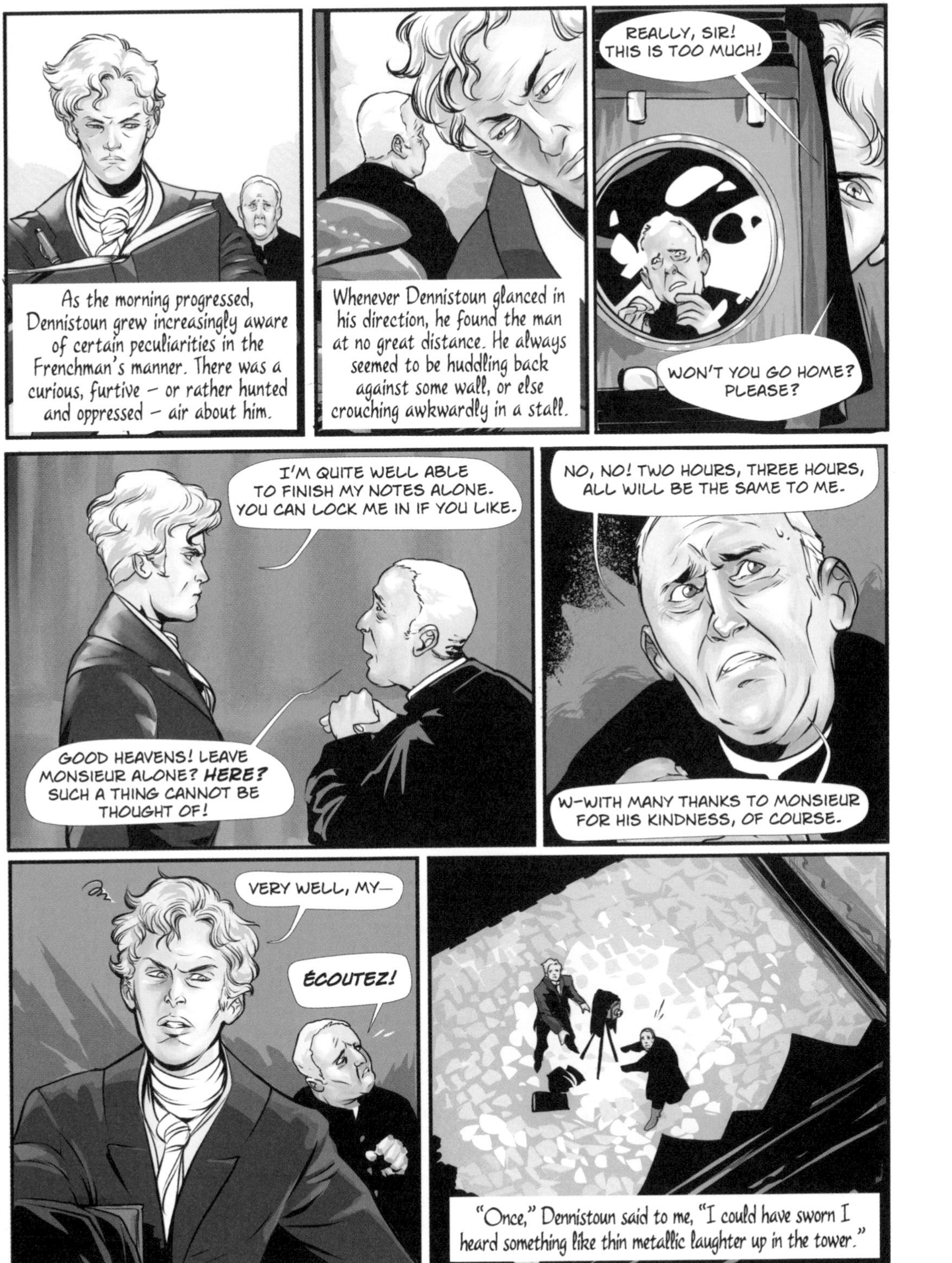
As the morning progressed, Dennistoun grew increasingly aware of certain peculiarities in the Frenchman's manner. There was a curious, furtive – or rather hunted and oppressed – air about him.
Whenever Dennistoun glanced in his direction, he found the man at no great distance. He always seemed to be huddling back against some wall, or else crouching awkwardly in a stall.
REALLY, SIR! THIS IS TOO MUCH!
WON'T YOU GO HOME? PLEASE?
I'M QUITE WELL ABLE TO FINISH MY NOTES ALONE. YOU CAN LOCK ME IN IF YOU LIKE.
GOOD HEAVENS! LEAVE MONSIEUR ALONE? **HERE?** SUCH A THING CANNOT BE THOUGHT OF!
NO, NO! TWO HOURS, THREE HOURS, ALL WILL BE THE SAME TO ME.
W-WITH MANY THANKS TO MONSIEUR FOR HIS KINDNESS, OF COURSE.
VERY WELL, MY—
ÉCOUTEZ!
"Once," Dennistoun said to me, "I could have sworn I heard something like thin metallic laughter up in the tower."

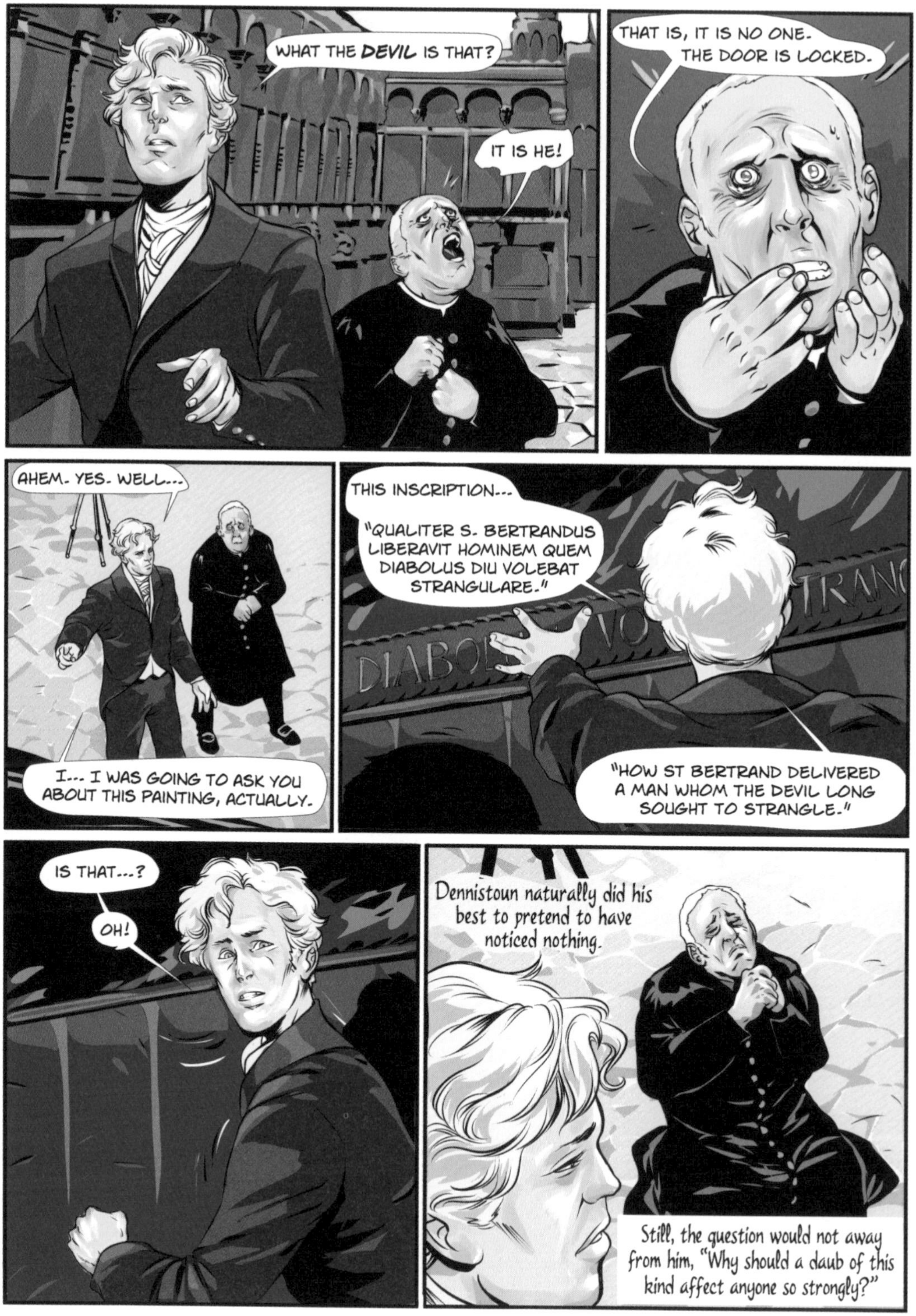
WHAT THE DEVIL IS THAT?
IT IS HE!
THAT IS, IT IS NO ONE. THE DOOR IS LOCKED.
AHEM. YES. WELL...
I... I WAS GOING TO ASK YOU ABOUT THIS PAINTING, ACTUALLY.
THIS INSCRIPTION...
"QUALITER S. BERTRANDUS LIBERAVIT HOMINEM QUEM DIABOLUS DIU VOLEBAT STRANGULARE."
"HOW ST BERTRAND DELIVERED A MAN WHOM THE DEVIL LONG SOUGHT TO STRANGLE."
IS THAT...?
OH!
Dennistoun naturally did his best to pretend to have noticed nothing.
Still, the question would not away from him, "Why should a daub of this kind affect anyone so strongly?"

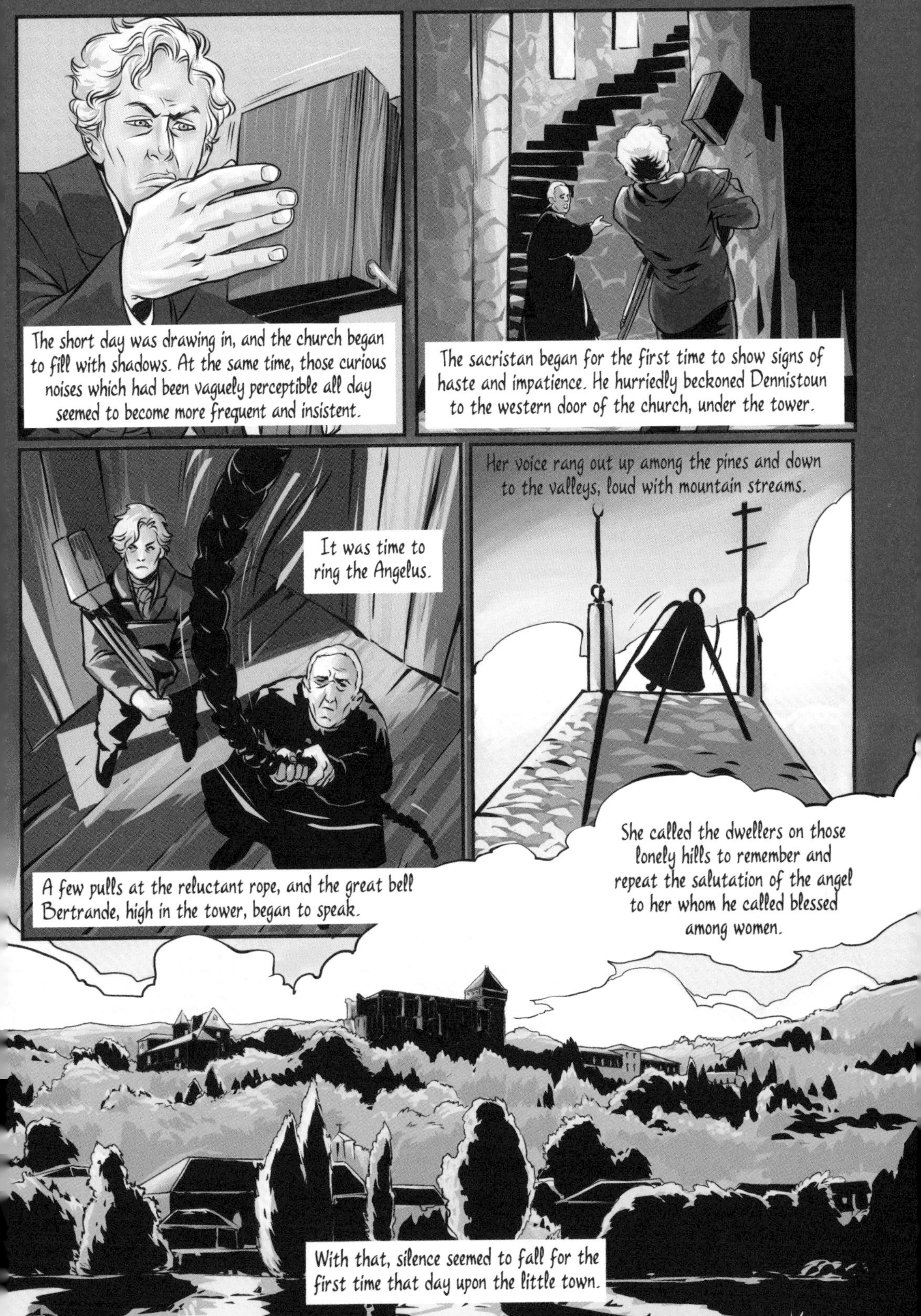
The short day was drawing in, and the church began to fill with shadows. At the same time, those curious noises which had been vaguely perceptible all day seemed to become more frequent and insistent.
The sacristan began for the first time to show signs of haste and impatience. He hurriedly beckoned Dennistoun to the western door of the church, under the tower.
It was time to ring the Angelus.
A few pulls at the reluctant rope, and the great bell Bertrande, high in the tower, began to speak.
Her voice rang out up among the pines and down to the valleys, loud with mountain streams.
She called the dwellers on those lonely hills to remember and repeat the salutation of the angel to her whom he called blessed among women.
With that, silence seemed to fall for the first time that day upon the little town.

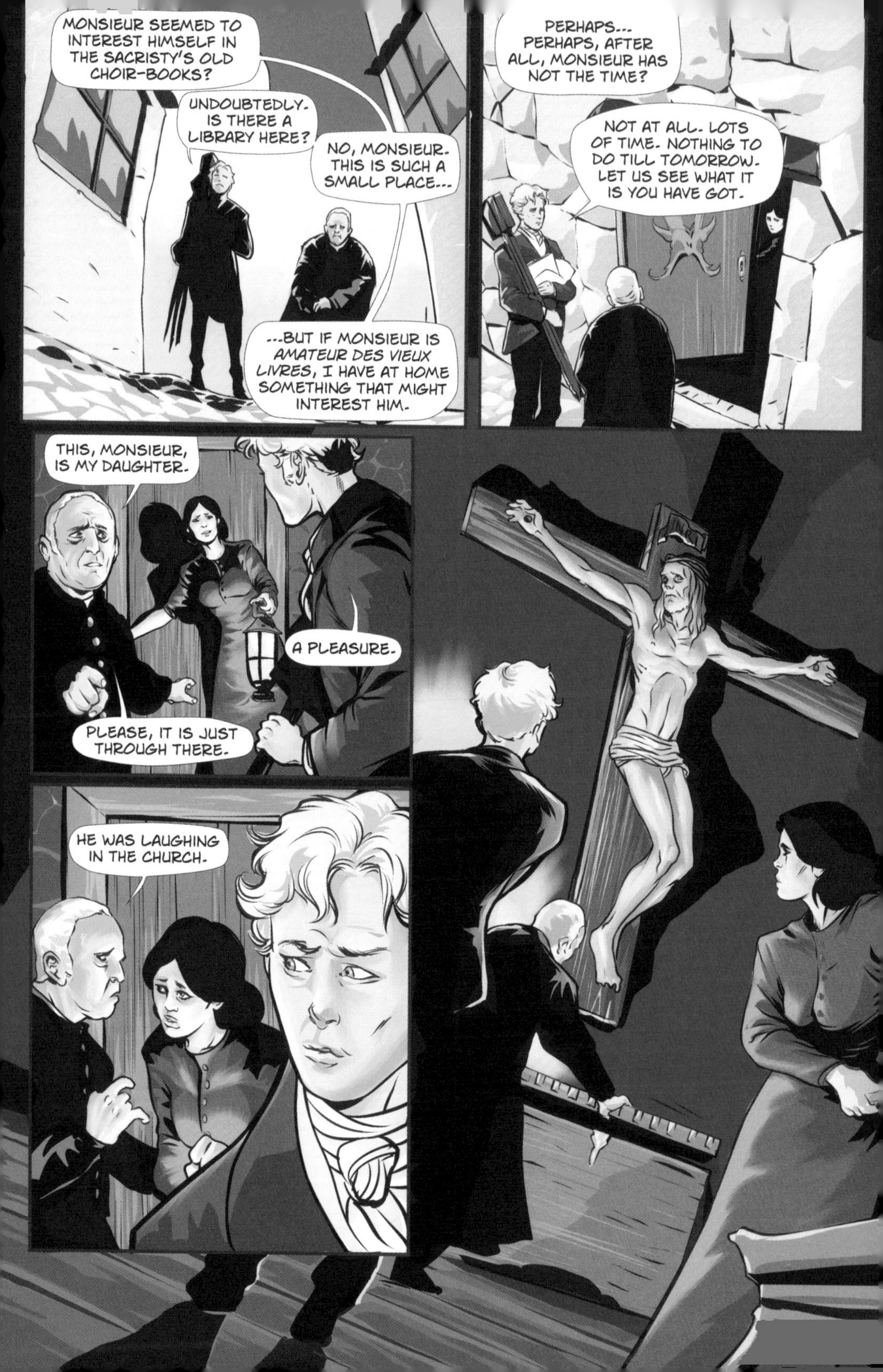
MONSIEUR SEEMED TO INTEREST HIMSELF IN THE SACRISTY'S OLD CHOIR-BOOKS?
UNDOUBTEDLY. IS THERE A LIBRARY HERE?
NO, MONSIEUR. THIS IS SUCH A SMALL PLACE...
...BUT IF MONSIEUR IS *AMATEUR DES VIEUX LIVRES*, I HAVE AT HOME SOMETHING THAT MIGHT INTEREST HIM.
PERHAPS... PERHAPS, AFTER ALL, MONSIEUR HAS NOT THE TIME?
NOT AT ALL. LOTS OF TIME. NOTHING TO DO TILL TOMORROW. LET US SEE WHAT IT IS YOU HAVE GOT.
THIS, MONSIEUR, IS MY DAUGHTER.
A PLEASURE.
PLEASE, IT IS JUST THROUGH THERE.
HE WAS LAUGHING IN THE CHURCH.

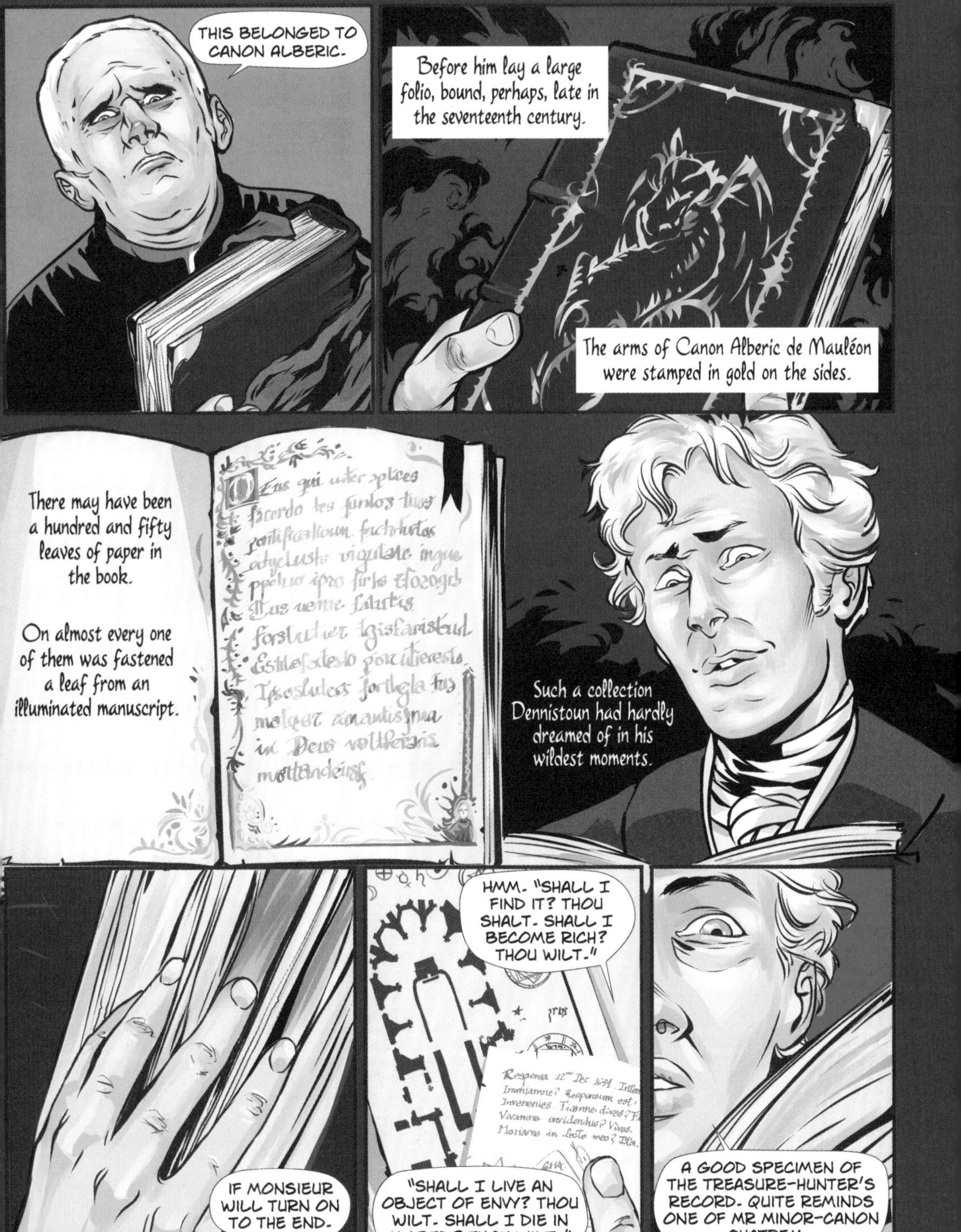
THIS BELONGED TO CANON ALBERIC.
Before him lay a large folio, bound, perhaps, late in the seventeenth century.
The arms of Canon Alberic de Mauléon were stamped in gold on the sides.
There may have been a hundred and fifty leaves of paper in the book.
On almost every one of them was fastened a leaf from an illuminated manuscript.
Such a collection Dennistoun had hardly dreamed of in his wildest moments.
IF MONSIEUR WILL TURN ON TO THE END.
HMM. "SHALL I FIND IT? THOU SHALT. SHALL I BECOME RICH? THOU WILT."
"SHALL I LIVE AN OBJECT OF ENVY? THOU WILT. SHALL I DIE IN MY BED? THOU WILT."
A GOOD SPECIMEN OF THE TREASURE-HUNTER'S RECORD. QUITE REMINDS ONE OF MR MINOR-CANON QUATREM—

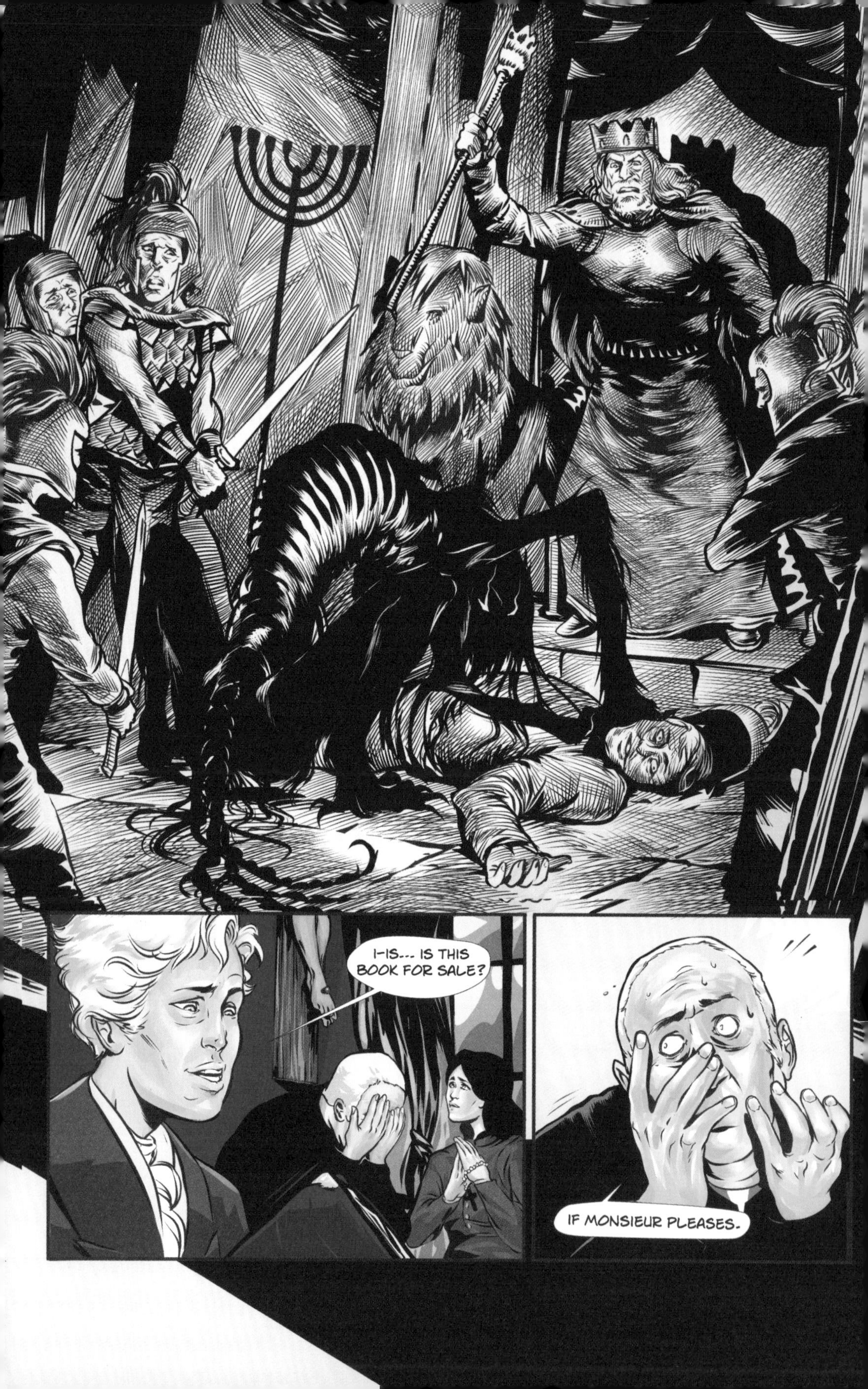
I-IS... IS THIS BOOK FOR SALE?
IF MONSIEUR PLEASES.

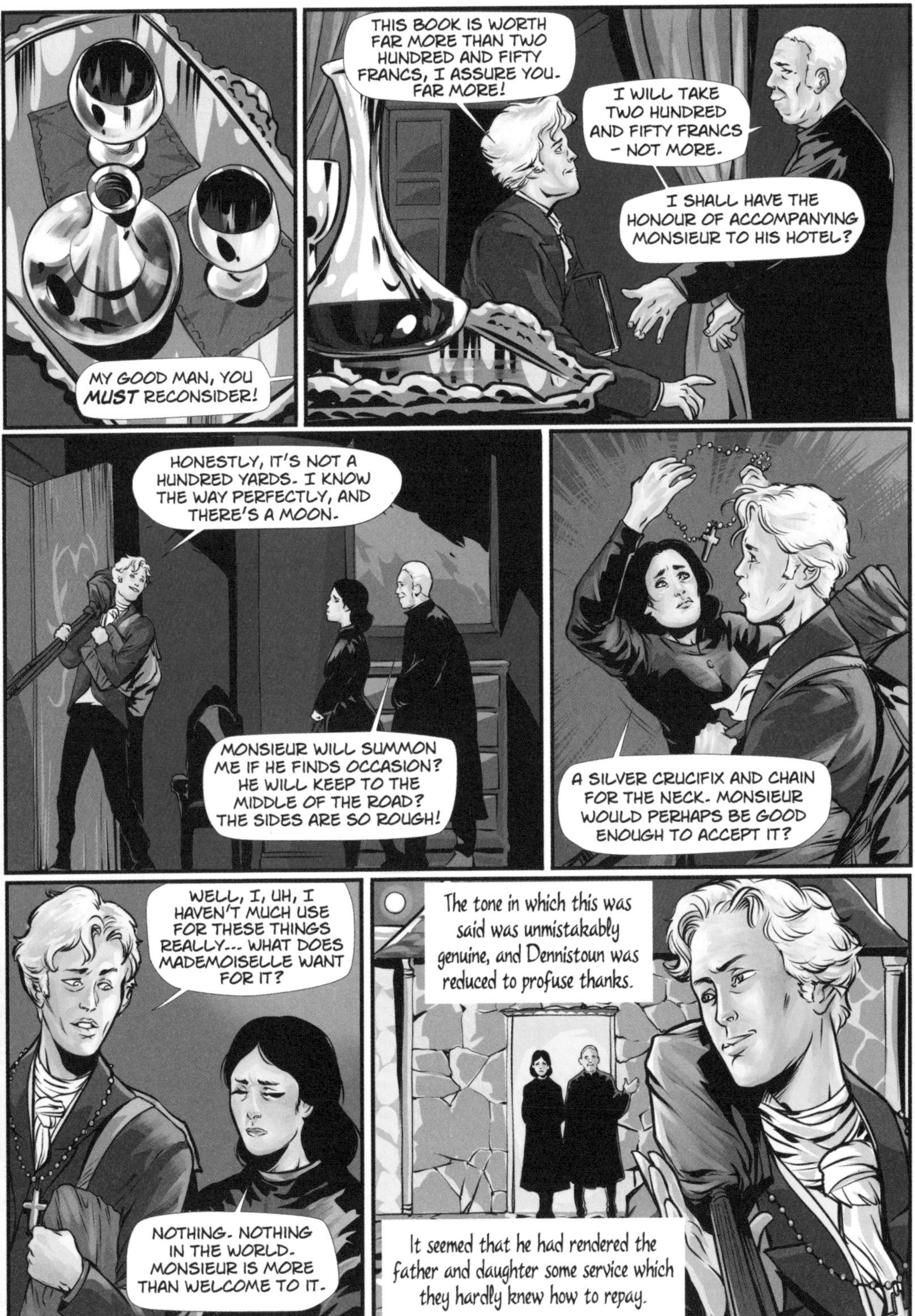
THIS BOOK IS WORTH FAR MORE THAN TWO HUNDRED AND FIFTY FRANCS, I ASSURE YOU. FAR MORE!
MY GOOD MAN, YOU MUST RECONSIDER!
I WILL TAKE TWO HUNDRED AND FIFTY FRANCS - NOT MORE.
I SHALL HAVE THE HONOUR OF ACCOMPANYING MONSIEUR TO HIS HOTEL?
HONESTLY, IT'S NOT A HUNDRED YARDS. I KNOW THE WAY PERFECTLY, AND THERE'S A MOON.
MONSIEUR WILL SUMMON ME IF HE FINDS OCCASION? HE WILL KEEP TO THE MIDDLE OF THE ROAD? THE SIDES ARE SO ROUGH!
A SILVER CRUCIFIX AND CHAIN FOR THE NECK. MONSIEUR WOULD PERHAPS BE GOOD ENOUGH TO ACCEPT IT?
WELL, I, UH, I HAVEN'T MUCH USE FOR THESE THINGS REALLY... WHAT DOES MADEMOISELLE WANT FOR IT?
NOTHING. NOTHING IN THE WORLD. MONSIEUR IS MORE THAN WELCOME TO IT.
The tone in which this was said was unmistakably genuine, and Dennistoun was reduced to profuse thanks.
It seemed that he had rendered the father and daughter some service which they hardly knew how to repay.

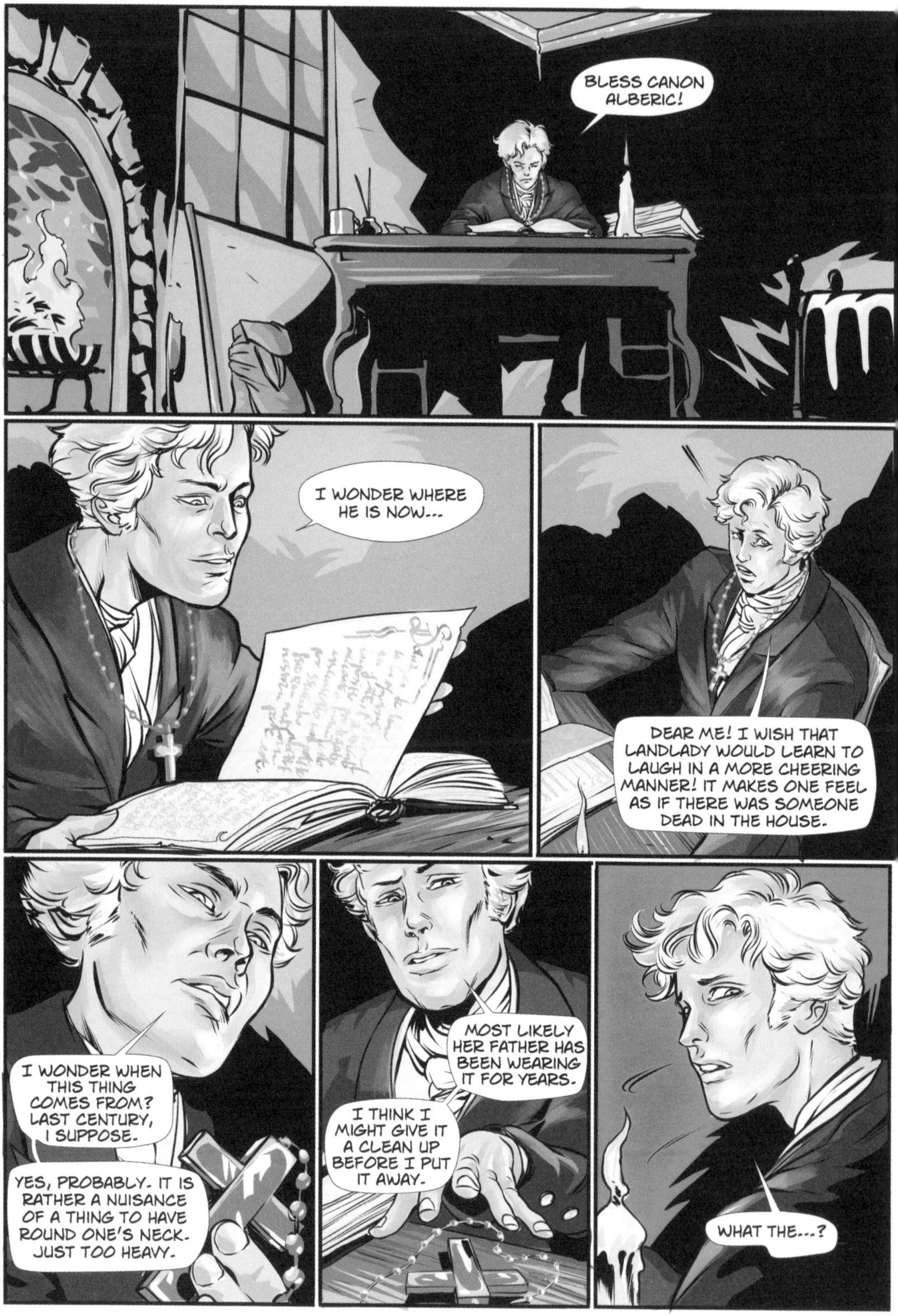
BLESS CANON ALBERIC!
I WONDER WHERE HE IS NOW...
DEAR ME! I WISH THAT LANDLADY WOULD LEARN TO LAUGH IN A MORE CHEERING MANNER! IT MAKES ONE FEEL AS IF THERE WAS SOMEONE DEAD IN THE HOUSE.
I WONDER WHEN THIS THING COMES FROM? LAST CENTURY, I SUPPOSE.
YES, PROBABLY. IT IS RATHER A NUISANCE OF A THING TO HAVE ROUND ONE'S NECK. JUST TOO HEAVY.
MOST LIKELY HER FATHER HAS BEEN WEARING IT FOR YEARS.
I THINK I MIGHT GIVE IT A CLEAN UP BEFORE I PUT IT AWAY.
WHAT THE...?

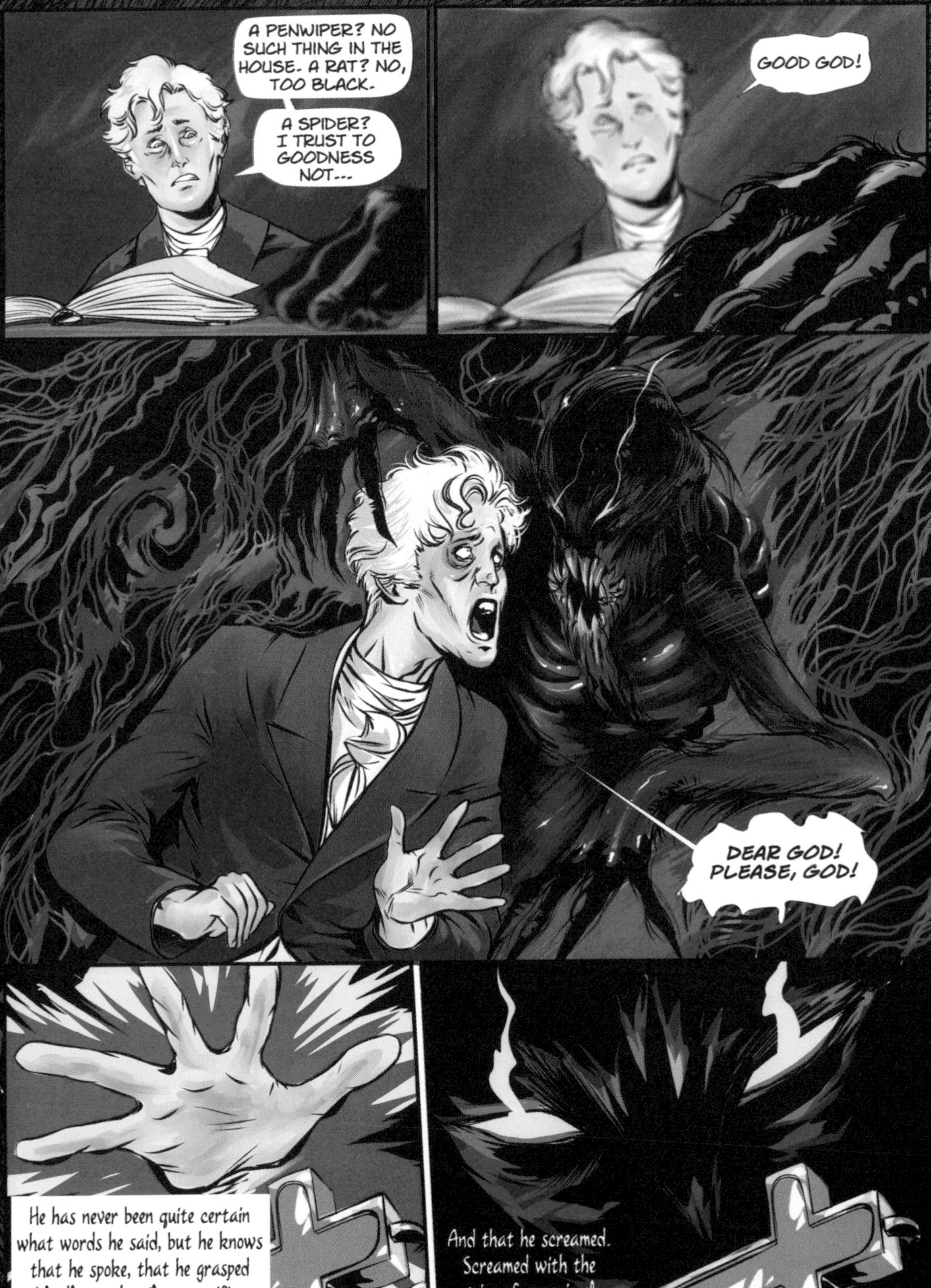
A PENWIPER? NO SUCH THING IN THE HOUSE. A RAT? NO, TOO BLACK.
A SPIDER? I TRUST TO GOODNESS NOT...
GOOD GOD!
DEAR GOD! PLEASE, GOD!
He has never been quite certain what words he said, but he knows that he spoke, that he grasped blindly at the silver crucifix.
And that he screamed. Screamed with the voice of an animal in hideous pain.

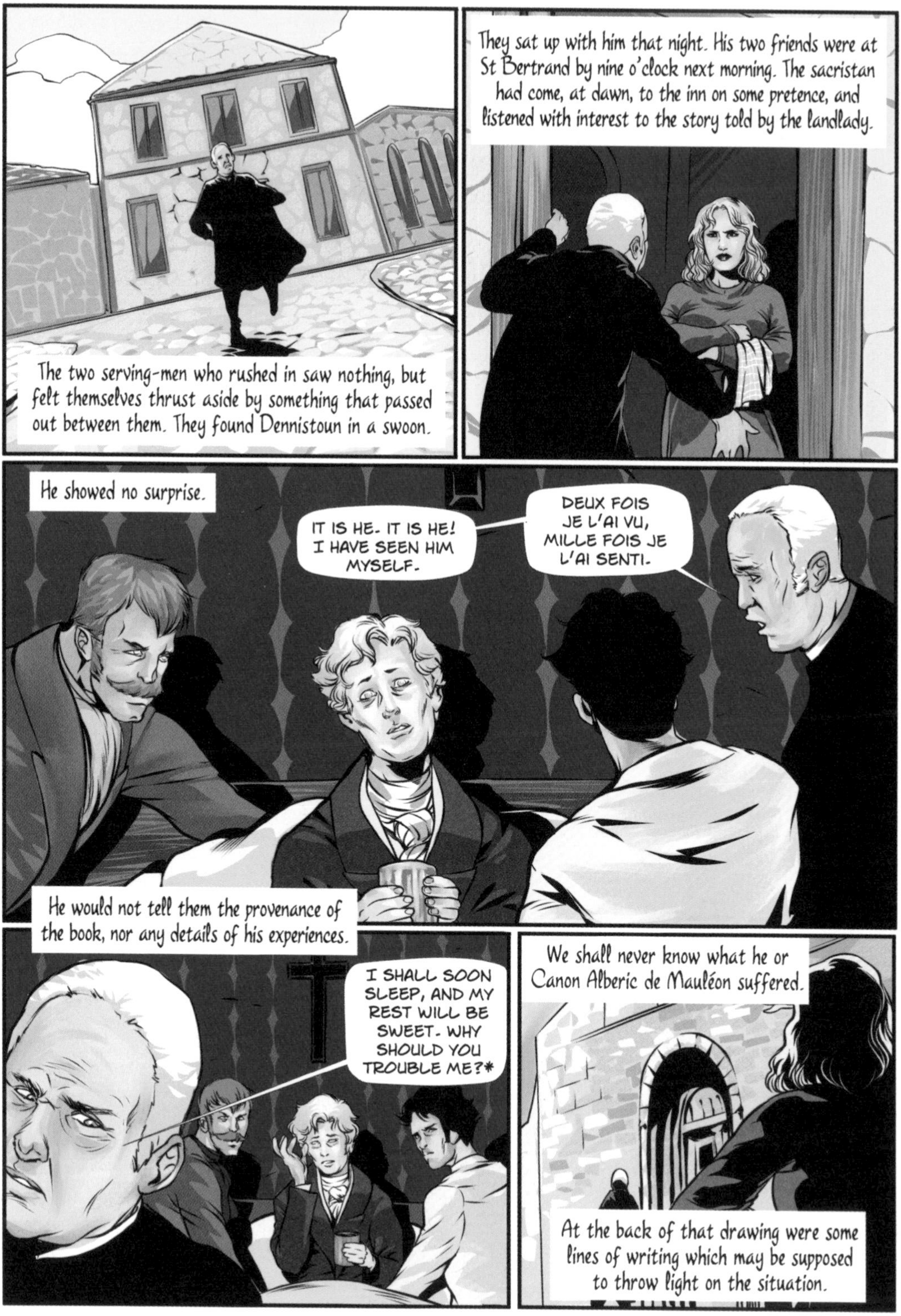
The two serving-men who rushed in saw nothing, but felt themselves thrust aside by something that passed out between them. They found Dennistoun in a swoon.
They sat up with him that night. His two friends were at St Bertrand by nine o'clock next morning. The sacristan had come, at dawn, to the inn on some pretence, and listened with interest to the story told by the landlady.
He showed no surprise.
IT IS HE. IT IS HE! I HAVE SEEN HIM MYSELF.
DEUX FOIS JE L'AI VU, MILLE FOIS JE L'AI SENTI.
He would not tell them the provenance of the book, nor any details of his experiences.
I SHALL SOON SLEEP, AND MY REST WILL BE SWEET. WHY SHOULD YOU TROUBLE ME?*
We shall never know what he or Canon Alberic de Mauléon suffered.
At the back of that drawing were some lines of writing which may be supposed to throw light on the situation.

* Footnote: He died that summer; his daughter married. She never understood the circumstances of her father's 'obsession'.

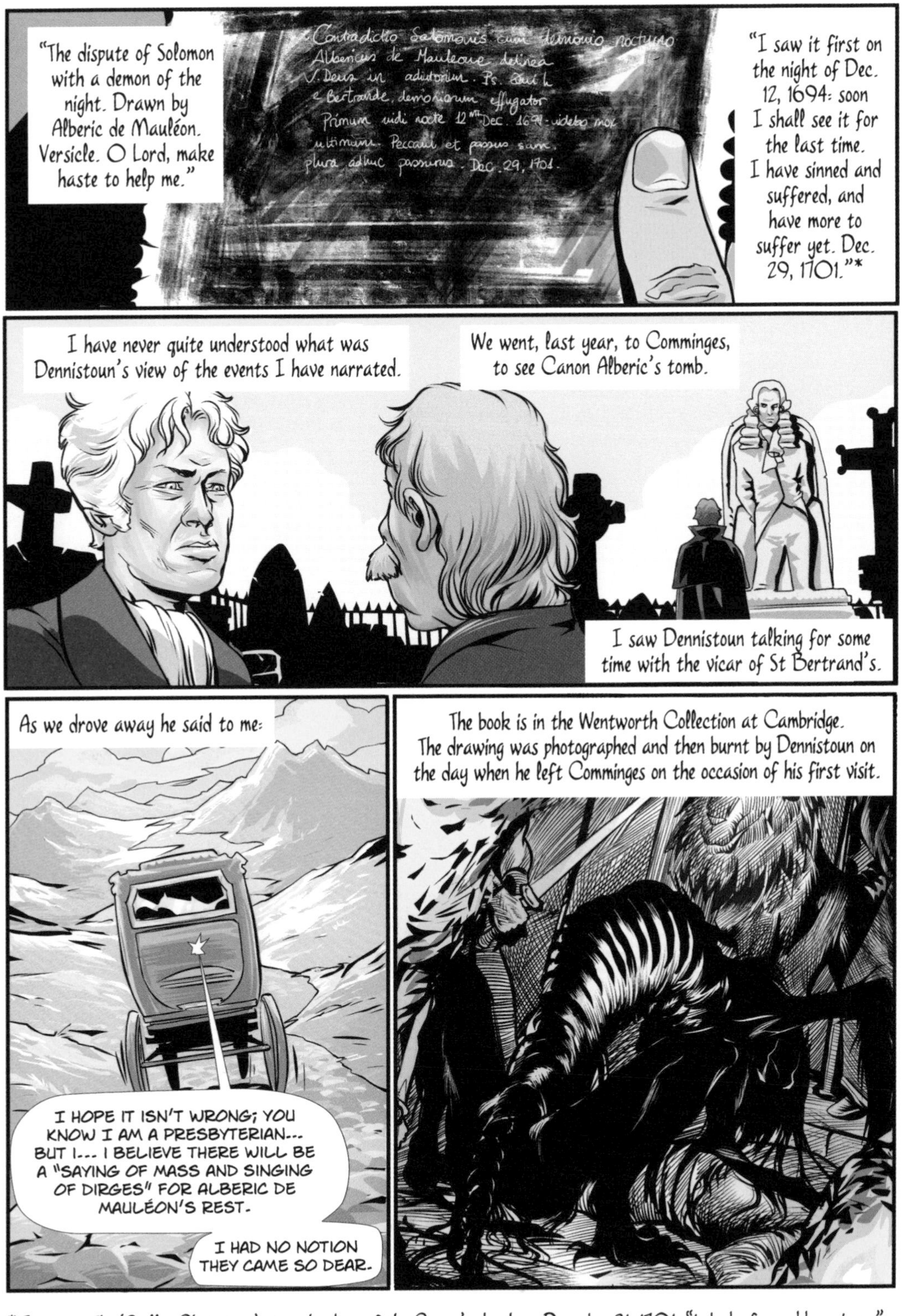
"The dispute of Solomon with a demon of the night. Drawn by Alberic de Mauléon. Versicle. O Lord, make haste to help me."
Contradictio Salomonis cum demonio nocturno
Albericus de Mauleone delinea
V. Deus in adiutorium. Ps. Qui h
e Bertrande, demoniorum effugator
Primum vidi nocte 12mi Dec. 1694 - videbo mox
ultimum. Peccavi et passus sum.
plura adhuc passurus. Dec. 29, 1701.
"I saw it first on the night of Dec. 12, 1694: soon I shall see it for the last time. I have sinned and suffered, and have more to suffer yet. Dec. 29, 1701."*
I have never quite understood what was Dennistoun's view of the events I have narrated.
We went, last year, to Comminges, to see Canon Alberic's tomb.
I saw Dennistoun talking for some time with the vicar of St Bertrand's.
As we drove away he said to me:
I HOPE IT ISN'T WRONG; YOU KNOW I AM A PRESBYTERIAN... BUT I... I BELIEVE THERE WILL BE A "SAYING OF MASS AND SINGING OF DIRGES" FOR ALBERIC DE MAULÉON'S REST.
I HAD NO NOTION THEY CAME SO DEAR.
The book is in the Wentworth Collection at Cambridge. The drawing was photographed and then burnt by Dennistoun on the day when he left Comminges on the occasion of his first visit.

* Footnote: The 'Gallia Christiana' gives the date of the Canon's death as December 31, 1701, "in bed, of a sudden seizure".

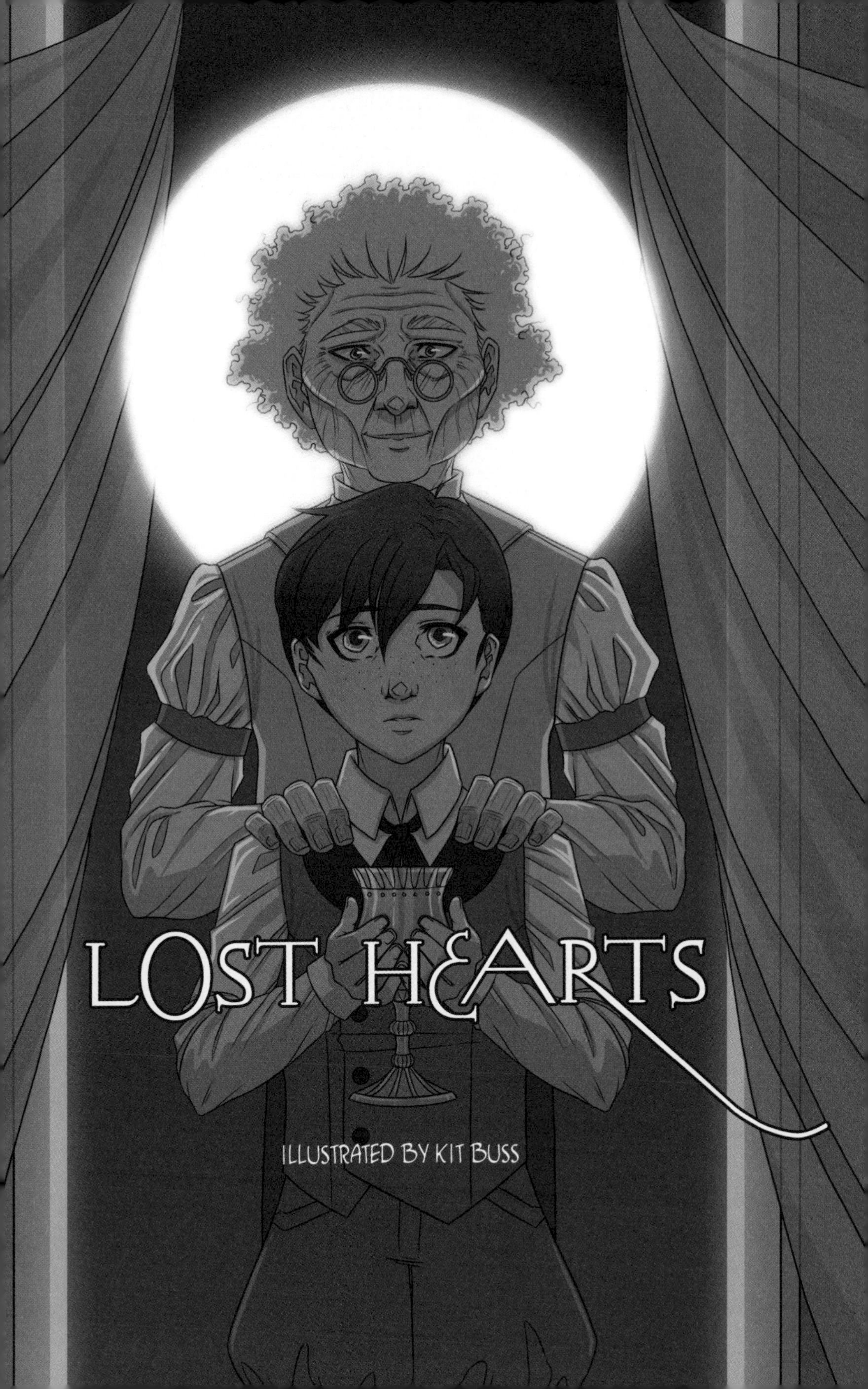
LOST HEARTS
ILLUSTRATED BY KIT BUSS

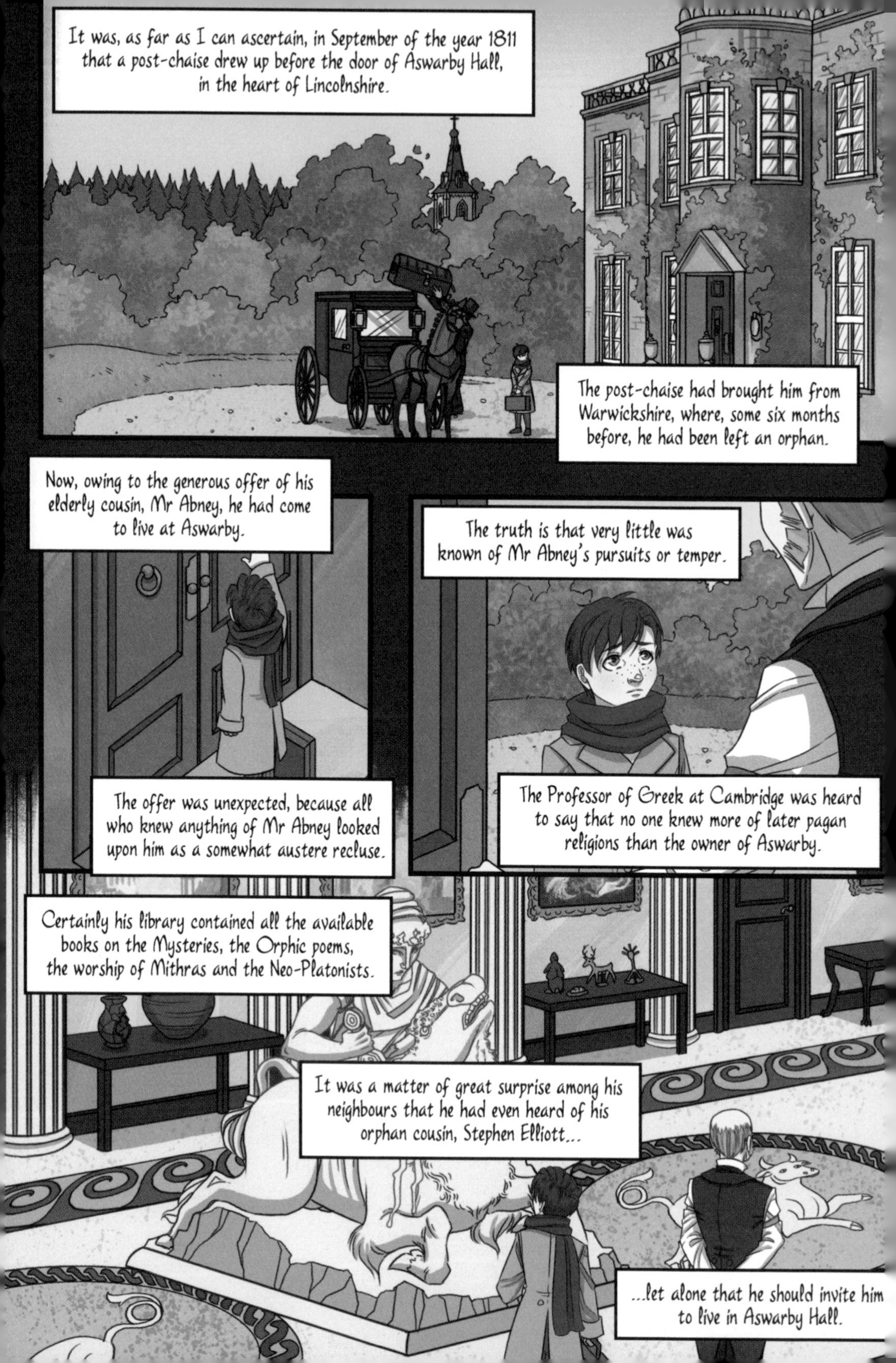
It was, as far as I can ascertain, in September of the year 1811 that a post-chaise drew up before the door of Aswarby Hall, in the heart of Lincolnshire.
The post-chaise had brought him from Warwickshire, where, some six months before, he had been left an orphan.
Now, owing to the generous offer of his elderly cousin, Mr Abney, he had come to live at Aswarby.
The offer was unexpected, because all who knew anything of Mr Abney looked upon him as a somewhat austere recluse.
The truth is that very little was known of Mr Abney's pursuits or temper.
The Professor of Greek at Cambridge was heard to say that no one knew more of later pagan religions than the owner of Aswarby.
Certainly his library contained all the available books on the Mysteries, the Orphic poems, the worship of Mithras and the Neo-Platonists.
It was a matter of great surprise among his neighbours that he had even heard of his orphan cousin, Stephen Elliott...
...let alone that he should invite him to live in Aswarby Hall.

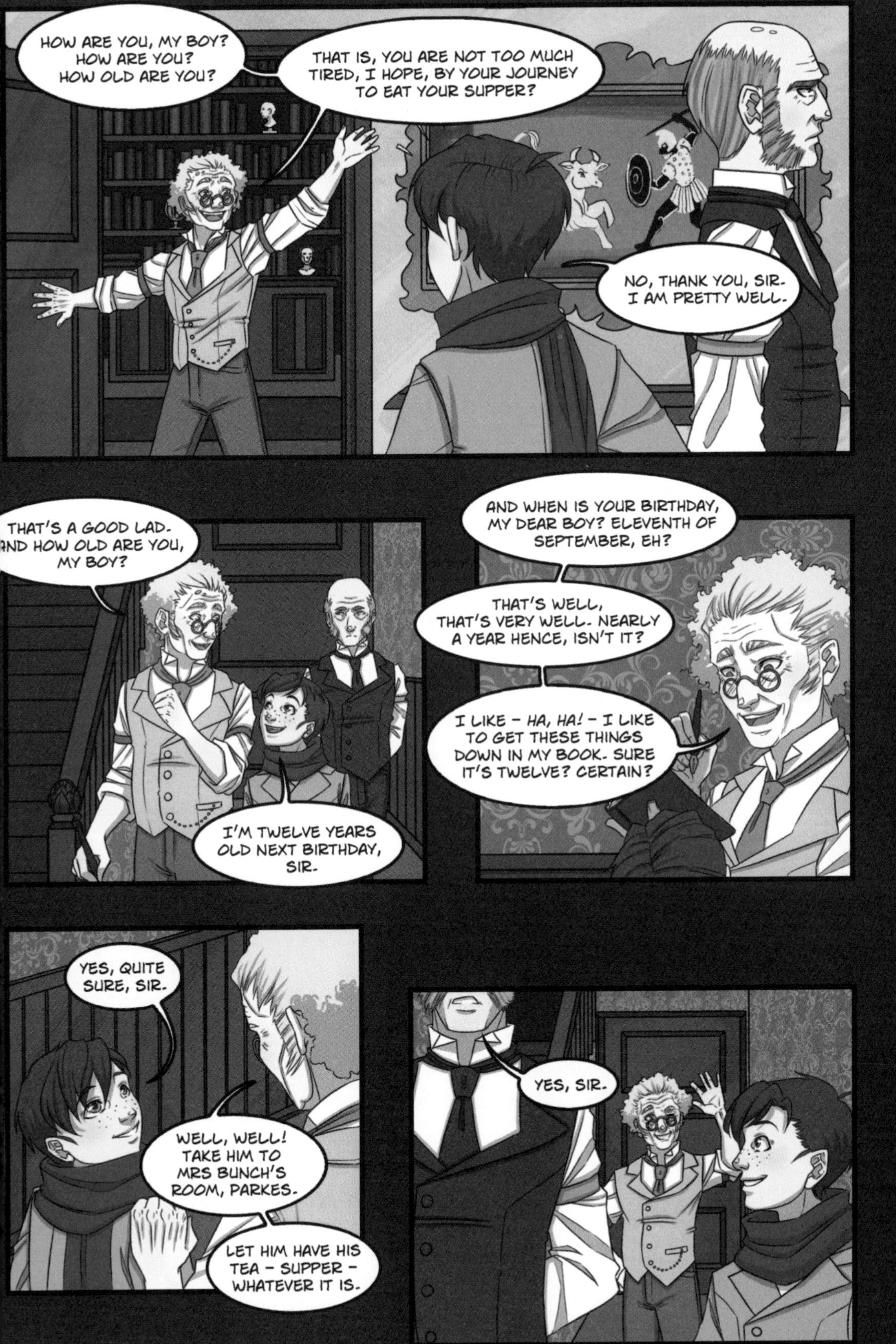
HOW ARE YOU, MY BOY? HOW ARE YOU? HOW OLD ARE YOU?
THAT IS, YOU ARE NOT TOO MUCH TIRED, I HOPE, BY YOUR JOURNEY TO EAT YOUR SUPPER?
NO, THANK YOU, SIR. I AM PRETTY WELL.
THAT'S A GOOD LAD. AND HOW OLD ARE YOU, MY BOY?
I'M TWELVE YEARS OLD NEXT BIRTHDAY, SIR.
AND WHEN IS YOUR BIRTHDAY, MY DEAR BOY? ELEVENTH OF SEPTEMBER, EH?
THAT'S WELL, THAT'S VERY WELL. NEARLY A YEAR HENCE, ISN'T IT?
I LIKE – HA, HA! – I LIKE TO GET THESE THINGS DOWN IN MY BOOK. SURE IT'S TWELVE? CERTAIN?
YES, QUITE SURE, SIR.
WELL, WELL! TAKE HIM TO MRS BUNCH'S ROOM, PARKES.
LET HIM HAVE HIS TEA – SUPPER – WHATEVER IT IS.
YES, SIR.

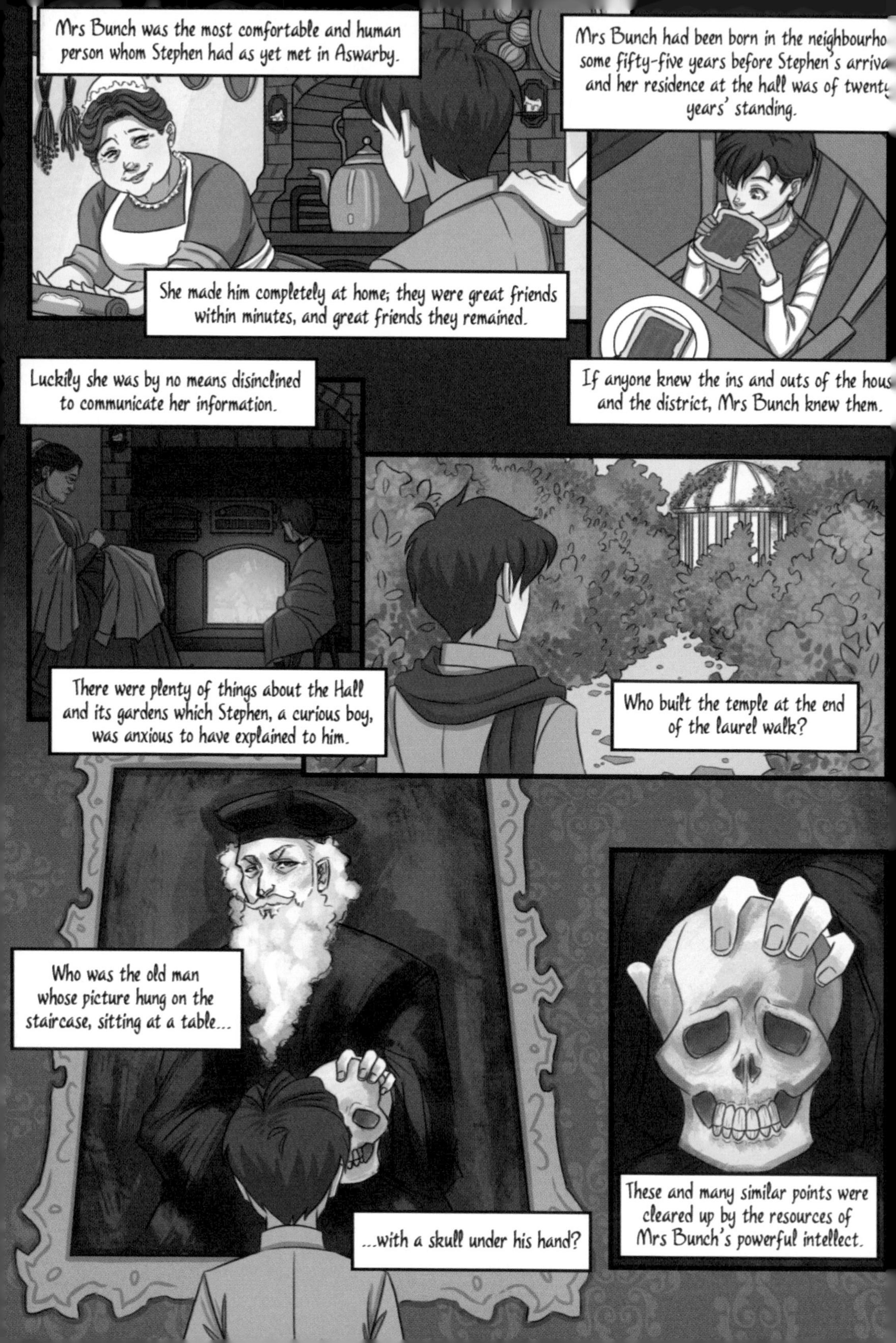
Mrs Bunch was the most comfortable and human person whom Stephen had as yet met in Aswarby.
Mrs Bunch had been born in the neighbourho some fifty-five years before Stephen's arriva and her residence at the hall was of twenty years' standing.
She made him completely at home; they were great friends within minutes, and great friends they remained.
Luckily she was by no means disinclined to communicate her information.
If anyone knew the ins and outs of the hous and the district, Mrs Bunch knew them.
There were plenty of things about the Hall and its gardens which Stephen, a curious boy, was anxious to have explained to him.
Who built the temple at the end of the laurel walk?
Who was the old man whose picture hung on the staircase, sitting at a table...
...with a skull under his hand?
These and many similar points were cleared up by the resources of Mrs Bunch's powerful intellect.

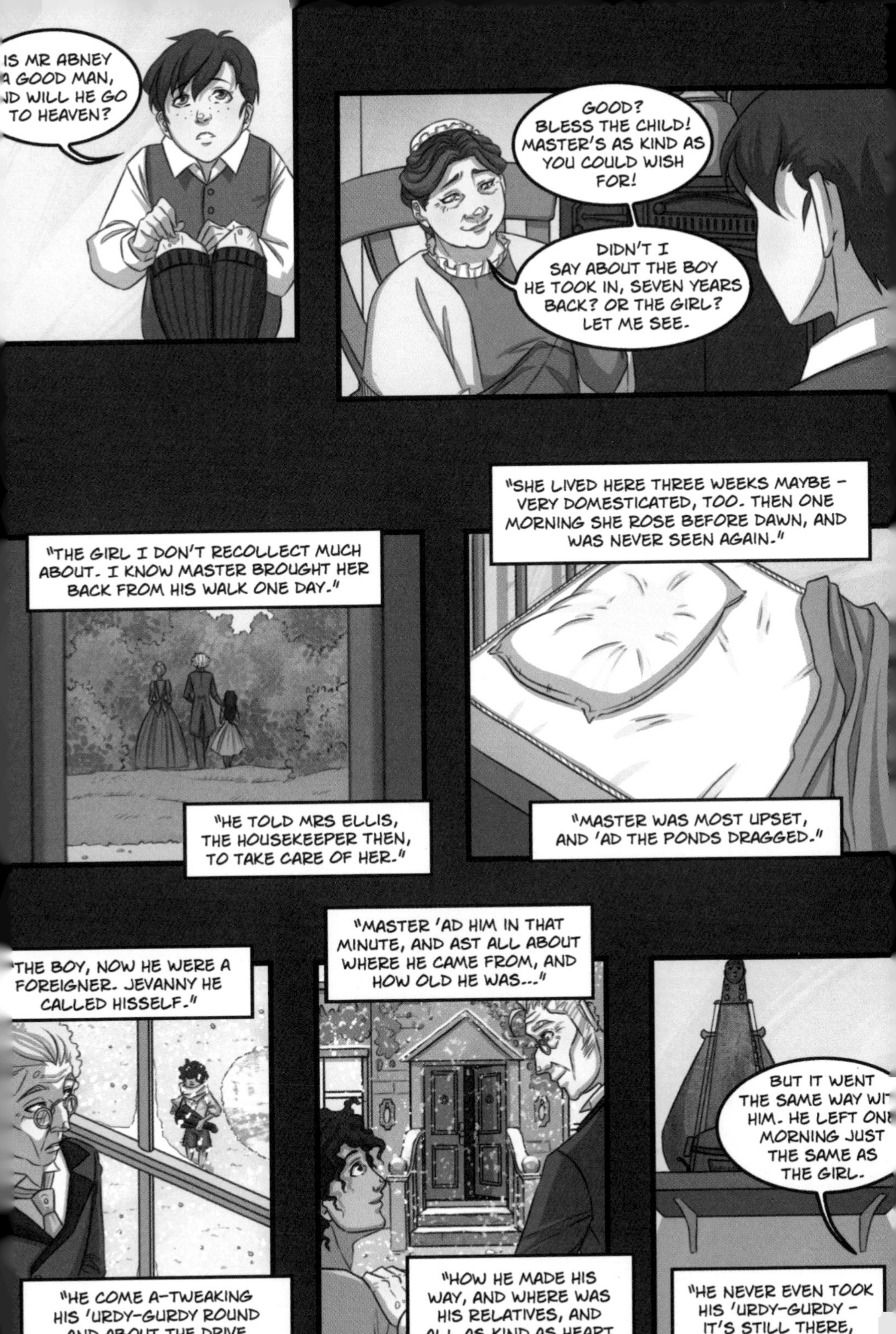

IS MR ABNEY A GOOD MAN, ND WILL HE GO TO HEAVEN?
GOOD? BLESS THE CHILD! MASTER'S AS KIND AS YOU COULD WISH FOR!
DIDN'T I SAY ABOUT THE BOY HE TOOK IN, SEVEN YEARS BACK? OR THE GIRL? LET ME SEE.
"THE GIRL I DON'T RECOLLECT MUCH ABOUT. I KNOW MASTER BROUGHT HER BACK FROM HIS WALK ONE DAY."
"HE TOLD MRS ELLIS, THE HOUSEKEEPER THEN, TO TAKE CARE OF HER."
"SHE LIVED HERE THREE WEEKS MAYBE – VERY DOMESTICATED, TOO. THEN ONE MORNING SHE ROSE BEFORE DAWN, AND WAS NEVER SEEN AGAIN."
"MASTER WAS MOST UPSET, AND 'AD THE PONDS DRAGGED."
"THE BOY, NOW HE WERE A FOREIGNER. JEVANNY HE CALLED HISSELF."
"HE COME A-TWEAKING HIS 'URDY-GURDY ROUND AND ABOUT THE DRIVE ONE WINTER DAY."
"MASTER 'AD HIM IN THAT MINUTE, AND AST ALL ABOUT WHERE HE CAME FROM, AND HOW OLD HE WAS..."
"HOW HE MADE HIS WAY, AND WHERE WAS HIS RELATIVES, AND ALL AS KIND AS HEART COULD WISH."
BUT IT WENT THE SAME WAY WI HIM. HE LEFT ON MORNING JUST THE SAME AS THE GIRL.
"HE NEVER EVEN TOOK HIS 'URDY-GURDY – IT'S STILL THERE, ON THE SHELF."

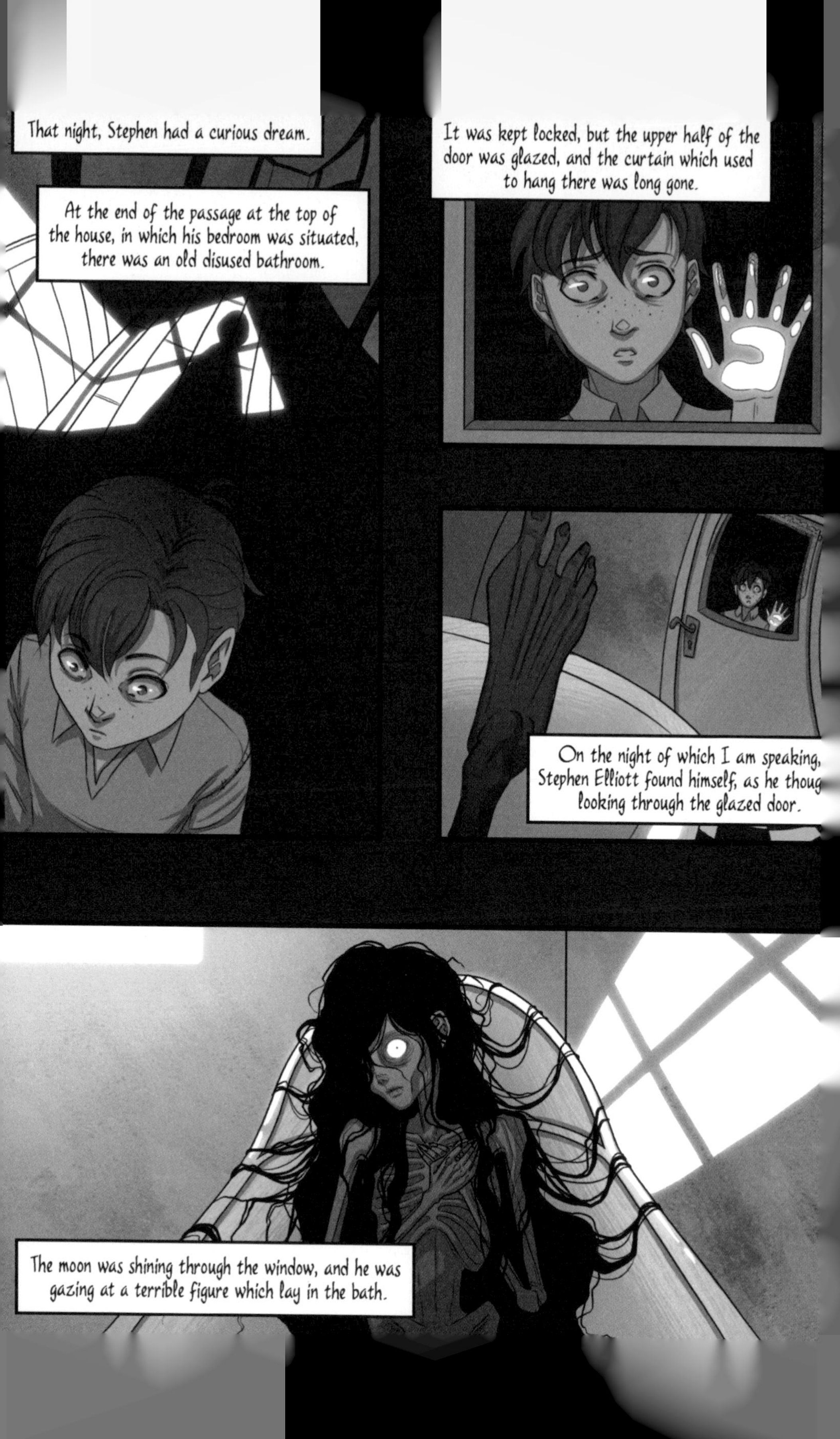
That night, Stephen had a curious dream.
At the end of the passage at the top of the house, in which his bedroom was situated, there was an old disused bathroom.
It was kept locked, but the upper half of the door was glazed, and the curtain which used to hang there was long gone.
On the night of which I am speaking, Stephen Elliott found himself, as he thoug looking through the glazed door.
The moon was shining through the window, and he was gazing at a terrible figure which lay in the bath.

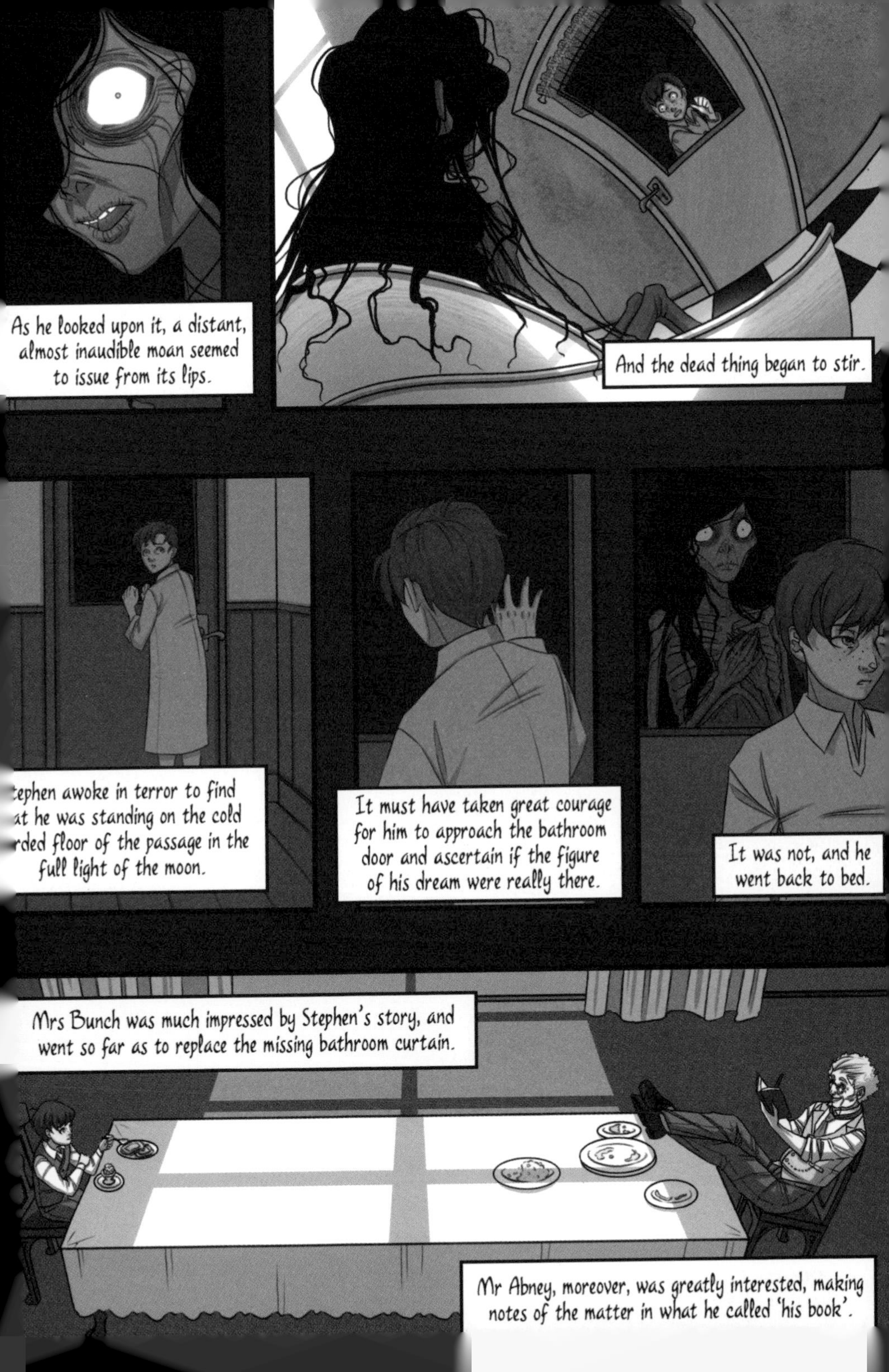
As he looked upon it, a distant, almost inaudible moan seemed to issue from its lips.
And the dead thing began to stir.
tephen awoke in terror to find at he was standing on the cold rded floor of the passage in the full light of the moon.
It must have taken great courage for him to approach the bathroom door and ascertain if the figure of his dream were really there.
It was not, and he went back to bed.
Mrs Bunch was much impressed by Stephen's story, and went so far as to replace the missing bathroom curtain.
Mr Abney, moreover, was greatly interested, making notes of the matter in what he called 'his book'.

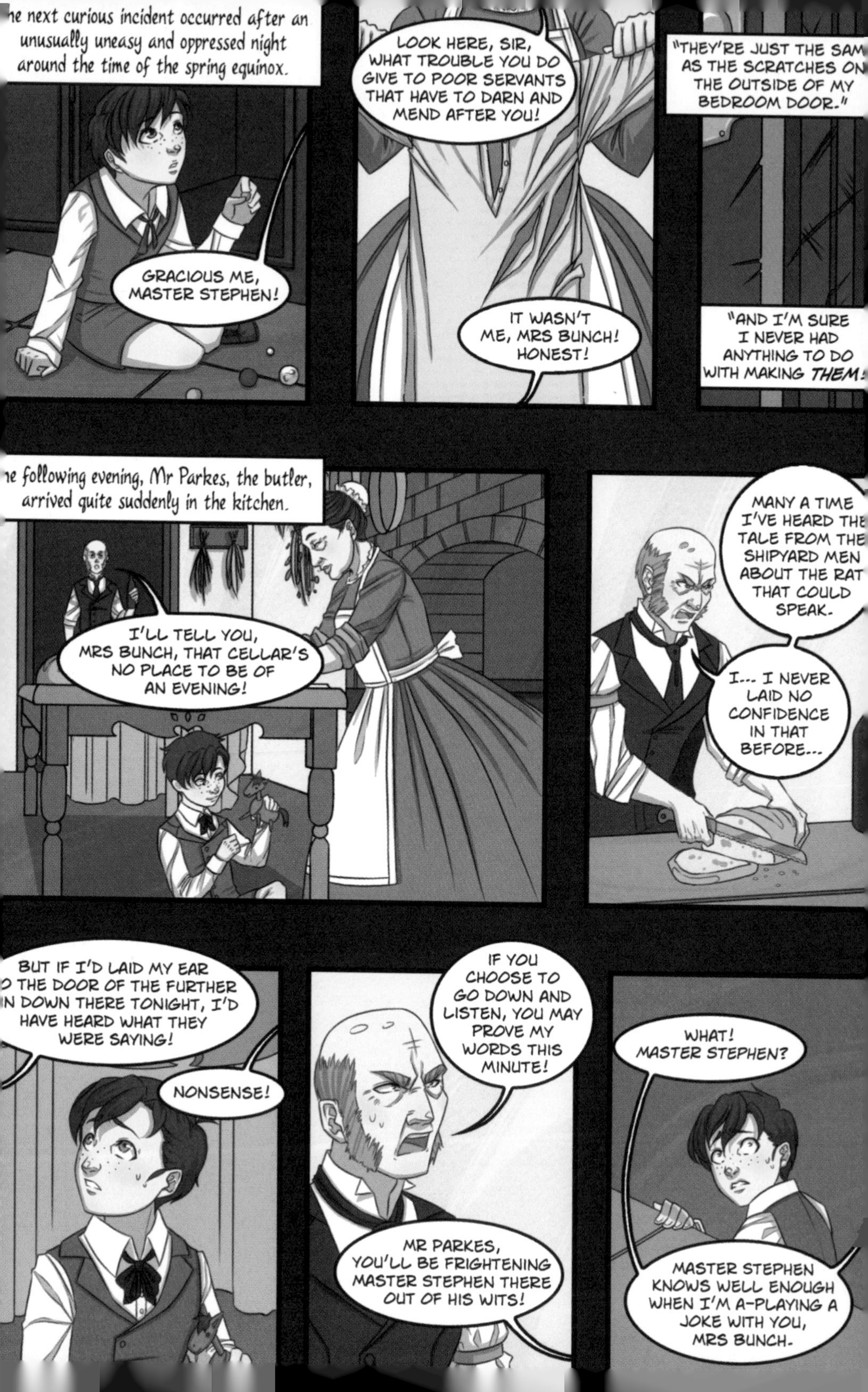
he next curious incident occurred after an unusually uneasy and oppressed night around the time of the spring equinox.
GRACIOUS ME, MASTER STEPHEN!
LOOK HERE, SIR, WHAT TROUBLE YOU DO GIVE TO POOR SERVANTS THAT HAVE TO DARN AND MEND AFTER YOU!
IT WASN'T ME, MRS BUNCH! HONEST!
"THEY'RE JUST THE SAM AS THE SCRATCHES ON THE OUTSIDE OF MY BEDROOM DOOR."
"AND I'M SURE I NEVER HAD ANYTHING TO DO WITH MAKING THEM."
he following evening, Mr Parkes, the butler, arrived quite suddenly in the kitchen.
I'LL TELL YOU, MRS BUNCH, THAT CELLAR'S NO PLACE TO BE OF AN EVENING!
MANY A TIME I'VE HEARD THE TALE FROM THE SHIPYARD MEN ABOUT THE RAT THAT COULD SPEAK.
I... I NEVER LAID NO CONFIDENCE IN THAT BEFORE...
BUT IF I'D LAID MY EAR O THE DOOR OF THE FURTHER N DOWN THERE TONIGHT, I'D HAVE HEARD WHAT THEY WERE SAYING!
NONSENSE!
IF YOU CHOOSE TO GO DOWN AND LISTEN, YOU MAY PROVE MY WORDS THIS MINUTE!
MR PARKES, YOU'LL BE FRIGHTENING MASTER STEPHEN THERE OUT OF HIS WITS!
WHAT! MASTER STEPHEN?
MASTER STEPHEN KNOWS WELL ENOUGH WHEN I'M A-PLAYING A JOKE WITH YOU, MRS BUNCH.

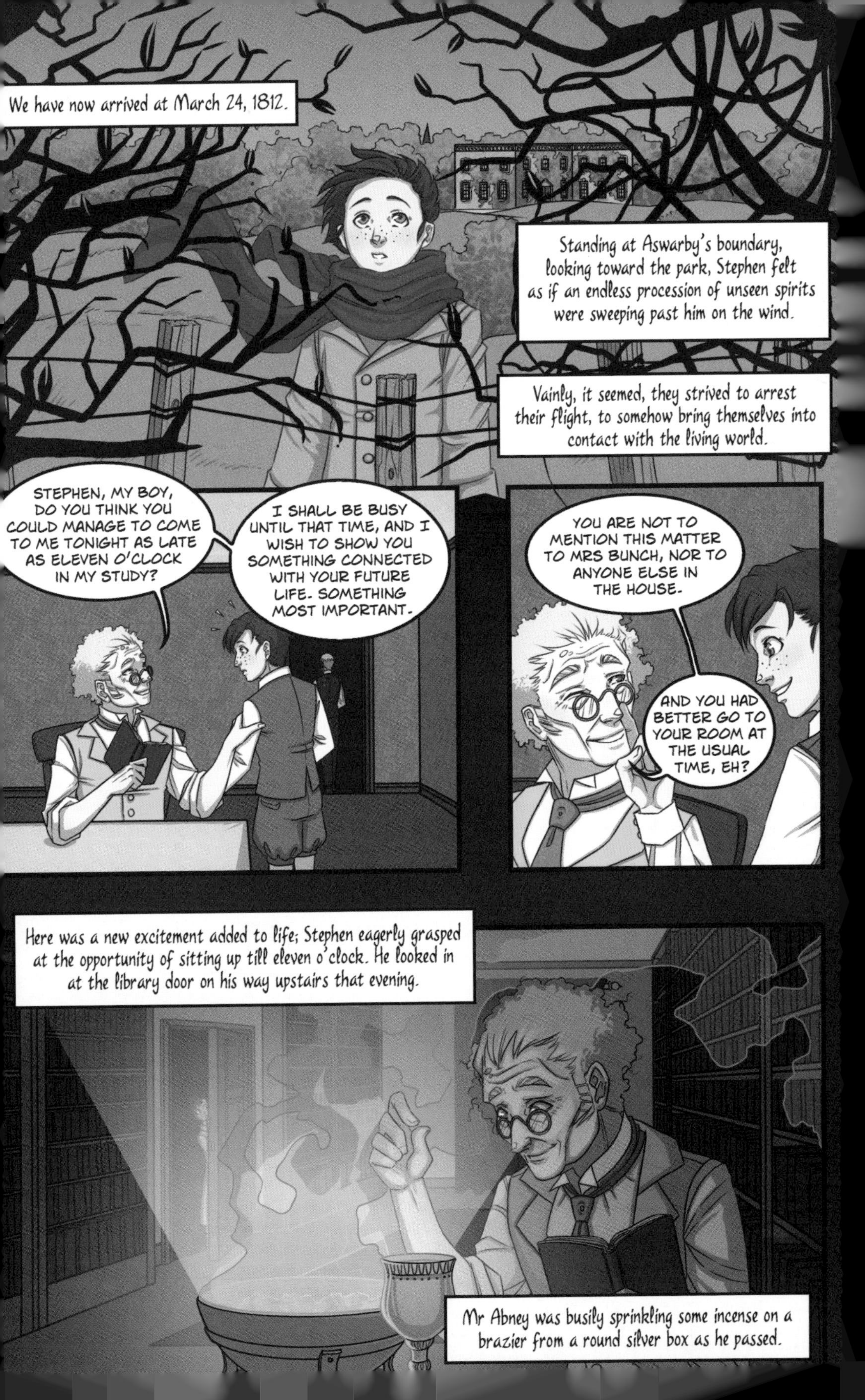
We have now arrived at March 24, 1812.
Standing at Aswarby's boundary, looking toward the park, Stephen felt as if an endless procession of unseen spirits were sweeping past him on the wind.
Vainly, it seemed, they strived to arrest their flight, to somehow bring themselves into contact with the living world.
STEPHEN, MY BOY, DO YOU THINK YOU COULD MANAGE TO COME TO ME TONIGHT AS LATE AS ELEVEN O'CLOCK IN MY STUDY?
I SHALL BE BUSY UNTIL THAT TIME, AND I WISH TO SHOW YOU SOMETHING CONNECTED WITH YOUR FUTURE LIFE. SOMETHING MOST IMPORTANT.
YOU ARE NOT TO MENTION THIS MATTER TO MRS BUNCH, NOR TO ANYONE ELSE IN THE HOUSE.
AND YOU HAD BETTER GO TO YOUR ROOM AT THE USUAL TIME, EH?
Here was a new excitement added to life; Stephen eagerly grasped at the opportunity of sitting up till eleven o'clock. He looked in at the library door on his way upstairs that evening.
Mr Abney was busily sprinkling some incense on a brazier from a round silver box as he passed.

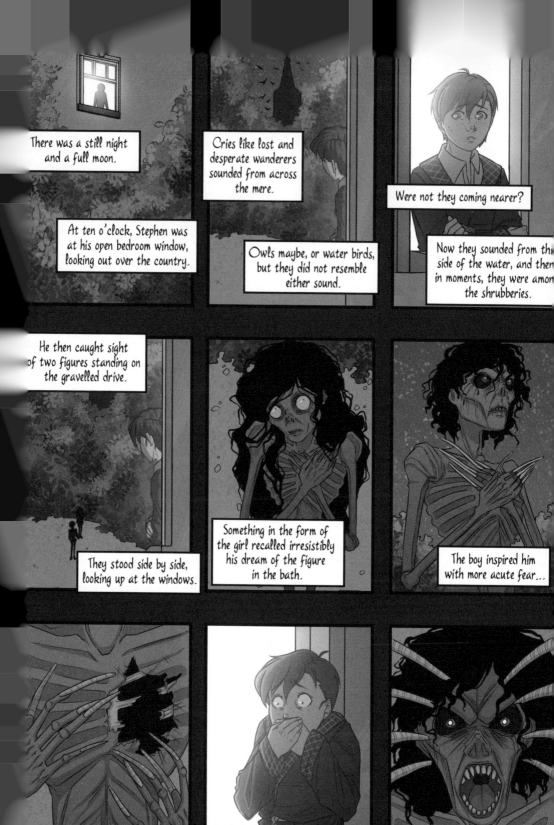

There was a still night and a full moon.

At ten o'clock, Stephen was at his open bedroom window, looking out over the country.

Cries like lost and desperate wanderers sounded from across the mere.

Owls maybe, or water birds, but they did not resemble either sound.

Were not they coming nearer?

Now they sounded from th[e] side of the water, and then in moments, they were amon[g] the shrubberies.

He then caught sight of two figures standing on the gravelled drive.

They stood side by side, looking up at the windows.

Something in the form of the girl recalled irresistibly his dream of the figure in the bath.

The boy inspired him with more acute fear...

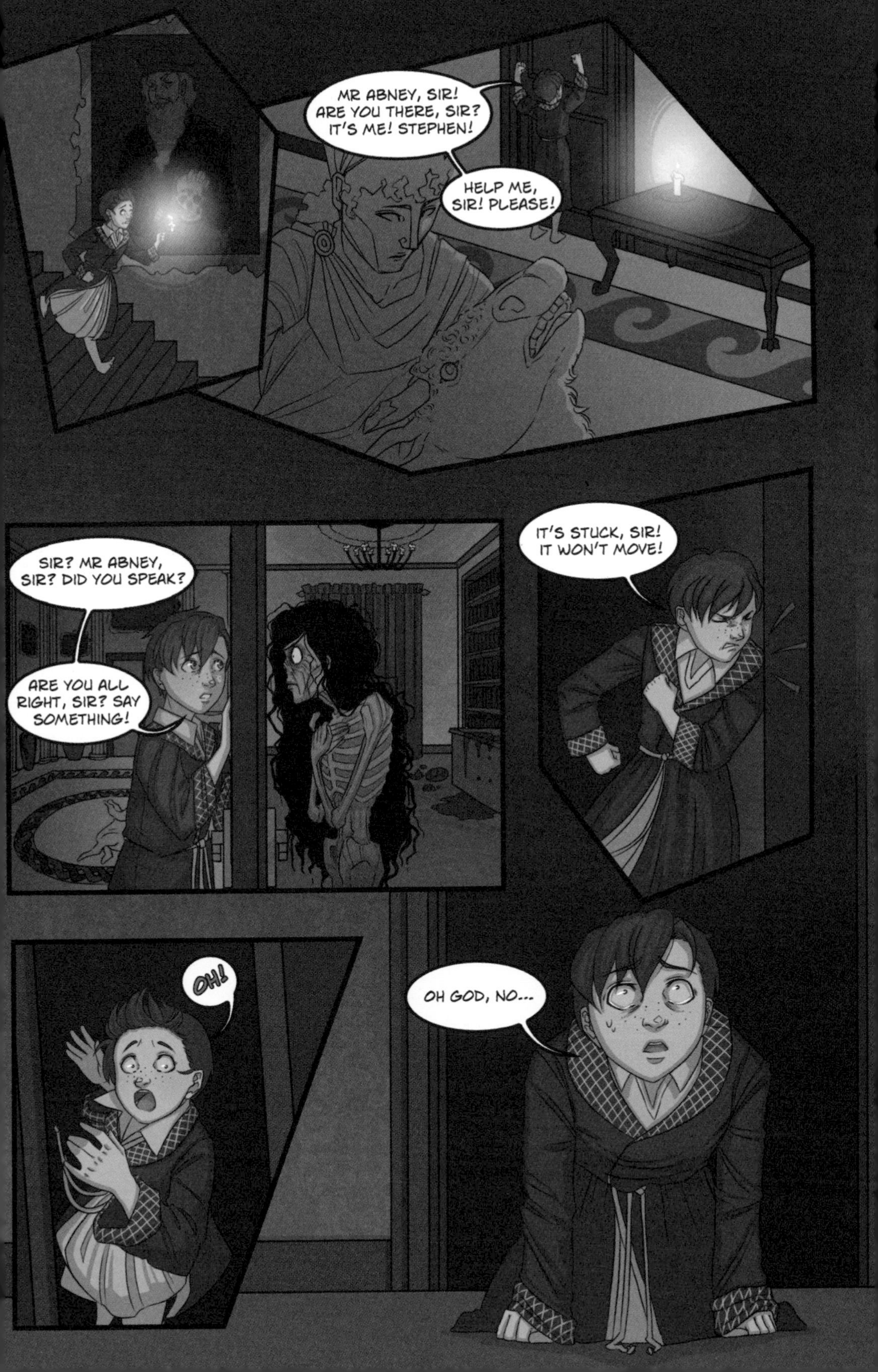
MR ABNEY, SIR! ARE YOU THERE, SIR? IT'S ME! STEPHEN!
HELP ME, SIR! PLEASE!
SIR? MR ABNEY, SIR? DID YOU SPEAK?
ARE YOU ALL RIGHT, SIR? SAY SOMETHING!
IT'S STUCK, SIR! IT WON'T MOVE!
OH!
OH GOD, NO...

Certain papers were found on Abney's table which explained the situation to Stephen Elliott when he was of an age to understand them:

The ancients believed that by absorbing a number of fellow-creatures...

...one may gain ascendancy over those spiritual beings which control the elemental forces.

Simon Magus is recorded as attaining his powers from a single life. Hermes Trismegistus, however, recommends no less than three.

Accordingly, then, I set the absorption of three hearts of less than twenty-one years as my personal objective.

The first step I effected by the removal of one Phoebe Stanley...

...a girl of gipsy extraction, on March 24, 1792.

The second, by the removal of a wandering Italian lad, named Giovanni Paoli, on the night of March 23, 1805.

The third must be my cousin, Stephen Elliott. His day must be this March 24, 1812.

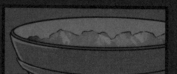

The best means of effecting the required absorption is to remove the heart from the living subject and reduce it to ashes.

The powder is then dissolved in about a pint of port or red wine and drunk down.

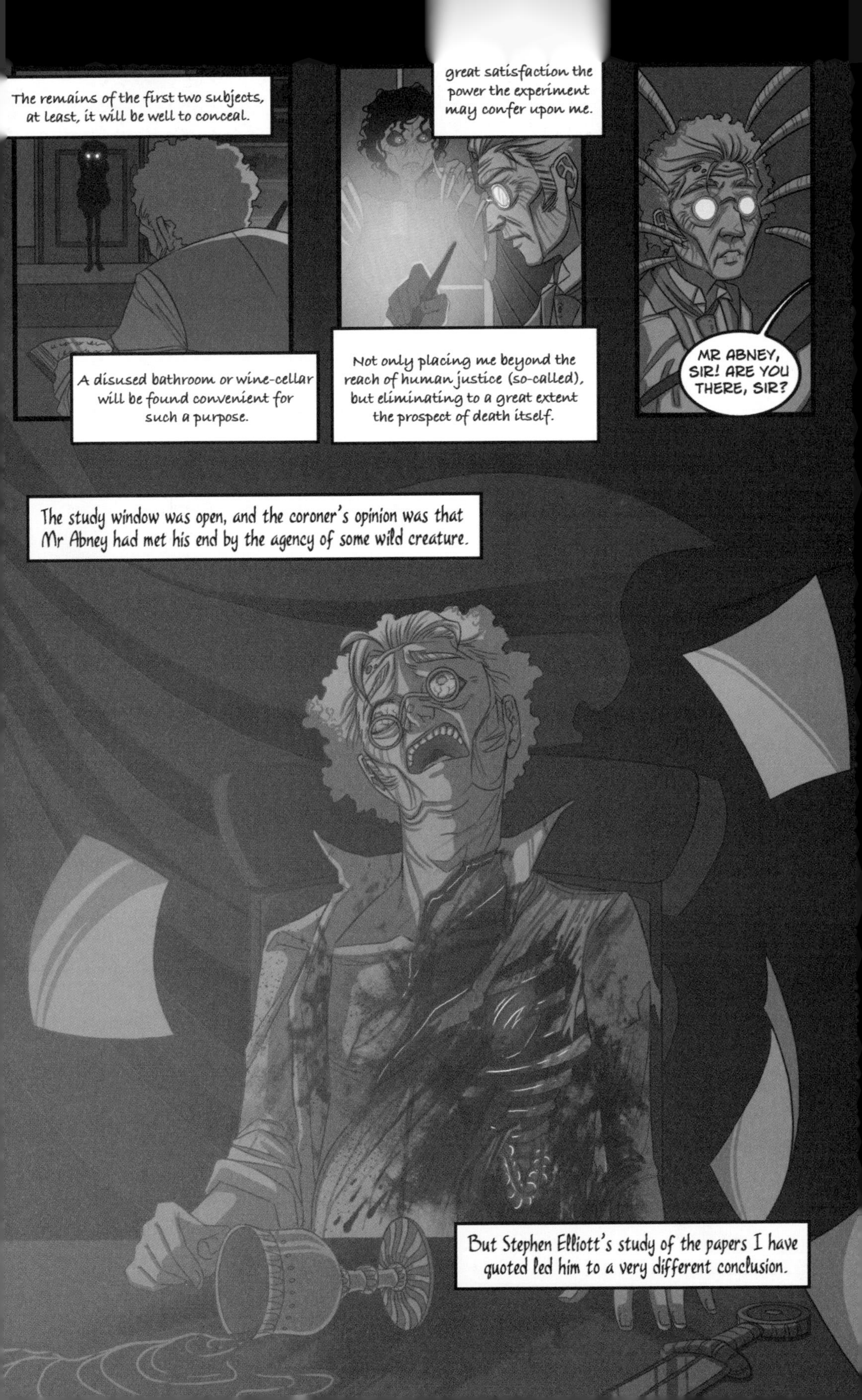
The remains of the first two subjects, at least, it will be well to conceal.
A disused bathroom or wine-cellar will be found convenient for such a purpose.
great satisfaction the power the experiment may confer upon me.
Not only placing me beyond the reach of human justice (so-called), but eliminating to a great extent the prospect of death itself.
MR ABNEY, SIR! ARE YOU THERE, SIR?
The study window was open, and the coroner's opinion was that Mr Abney had met his end by the agency of some wild creature.
But Stephen Elliott's study of the papers I have quoted led him to a very different conclusion.

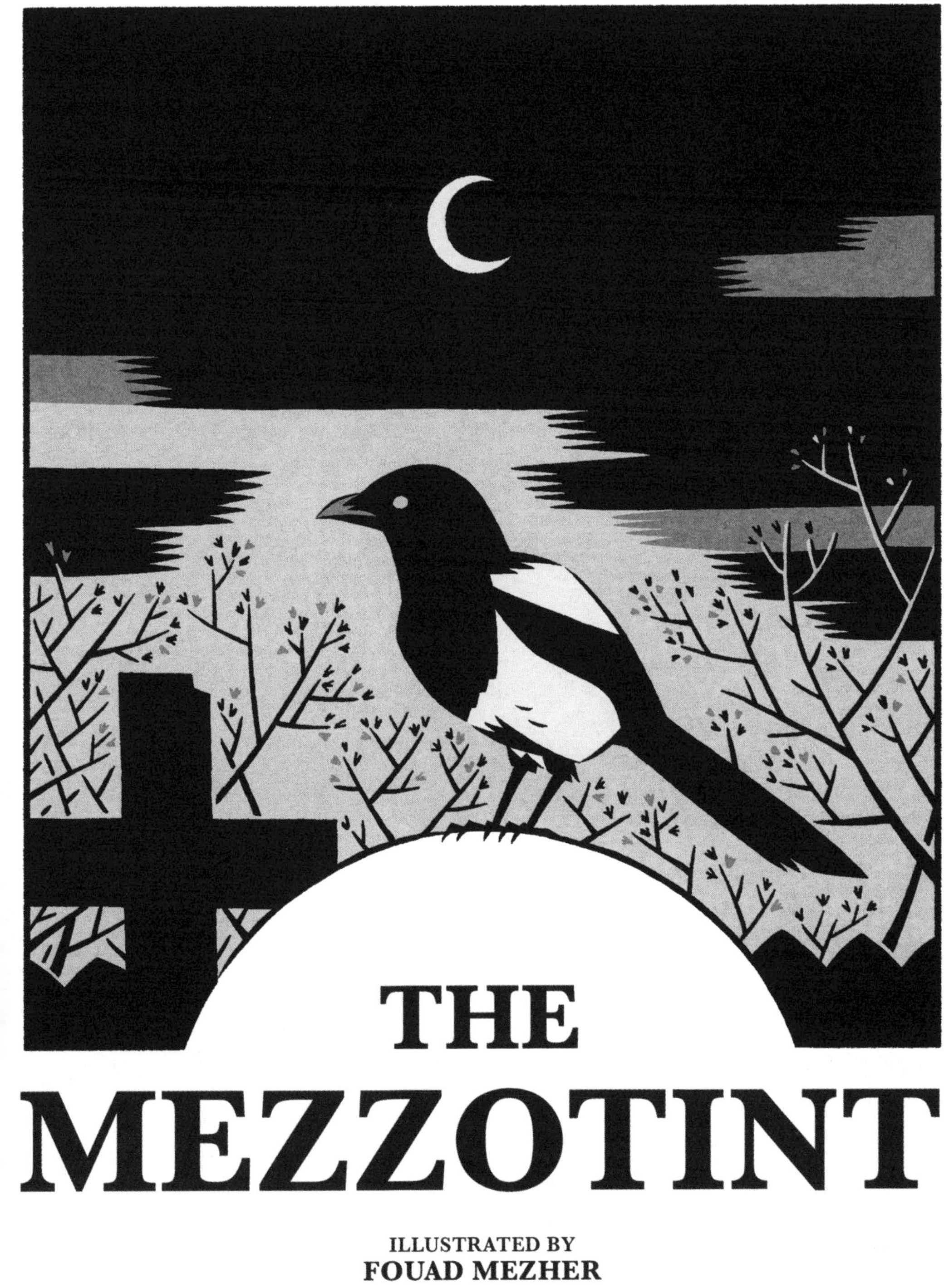

THE MEZZOTINT

ILLUSTRATED BY
FOUAD MEZHER

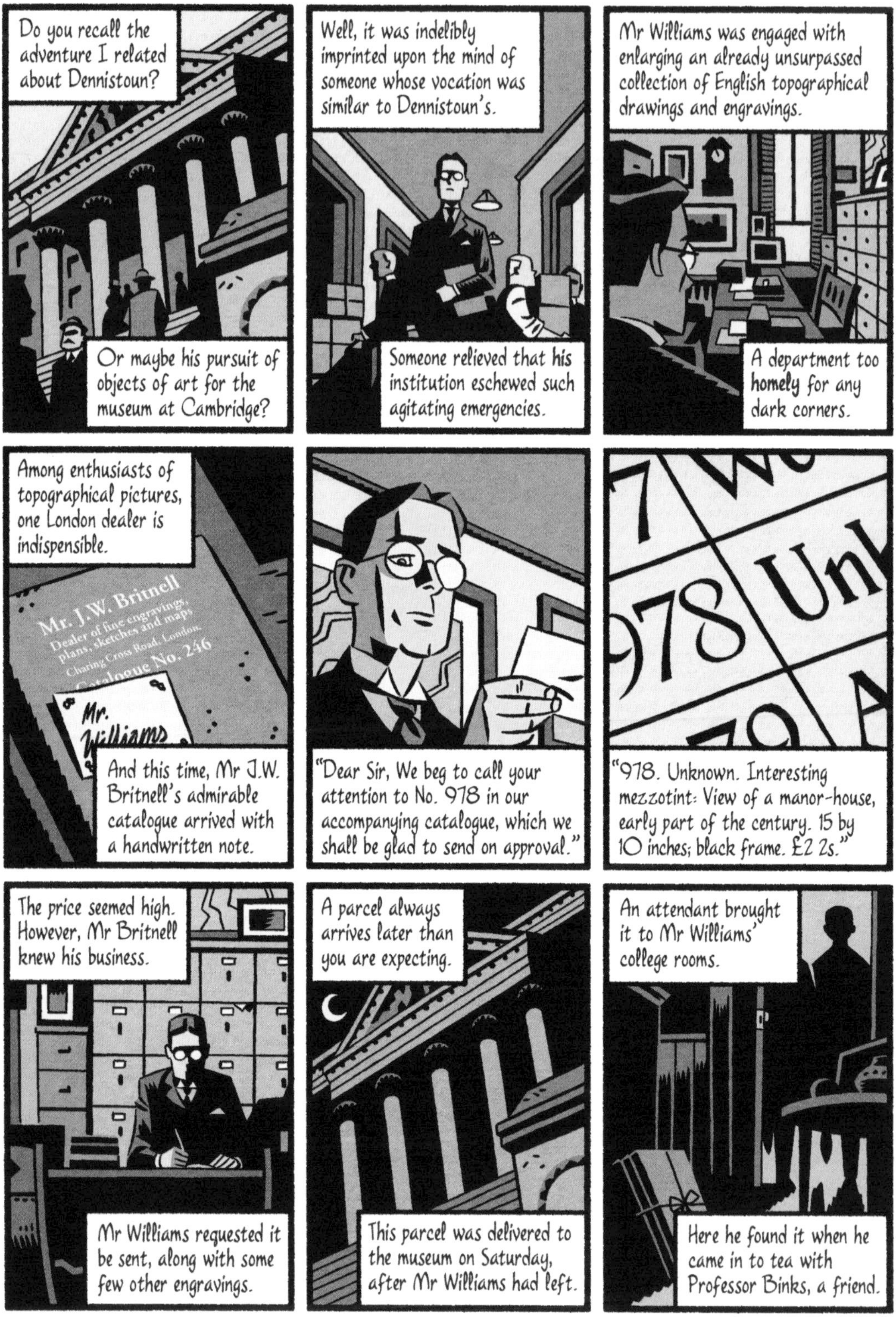
Do you recall the adventure I related about Dennistoun?
Or maybe his pursuit of objects of art for the museum at Cambridge?
Well, it was indelibly imprinted upon the mind of someone whose vocation was similar to Dennistoun's.
Someone relieved that his institution eschewed such agitating emergencies.
Mr Williams was engaged with enlarging an already unsurpassed collection of English topographical drawings and engravings.
A department too **homely** for any dark corners.
Among enthusiasts of topographical pictures, one London dealer is indispensible.
Mr. J.W. Britnell
Dealer of fine engravings, plans, sketches and maps
Charing Cross Road, London.
Catalogue No. 246
Mr. Williams
And this time, Mr J.W. Britnell's admirable catalogue arrived with a handwritten note.
"Dear Sir, We beg to call your attention to No. 978 in our accompanying catalogue, which we shall be glad to send on approval."
978
Unk
"978. Unknown. Interesting mezzotint: View of a manor-house, early part of the century. 15 by 10 inches; black frame. £2 2s."
The price seemed high. However, Mr Britnell knew his business.
Mr Williams requested it be sent, along with some few other engravings.
A parcel always arrives later than you are expecting.
This parcel was delivered to the museum on Saturday, after Mr Williams had left.
An attendant brought it to Mr Williams' college rooms.
Here he found it when he came in to tea with Professor Binks, a friend.

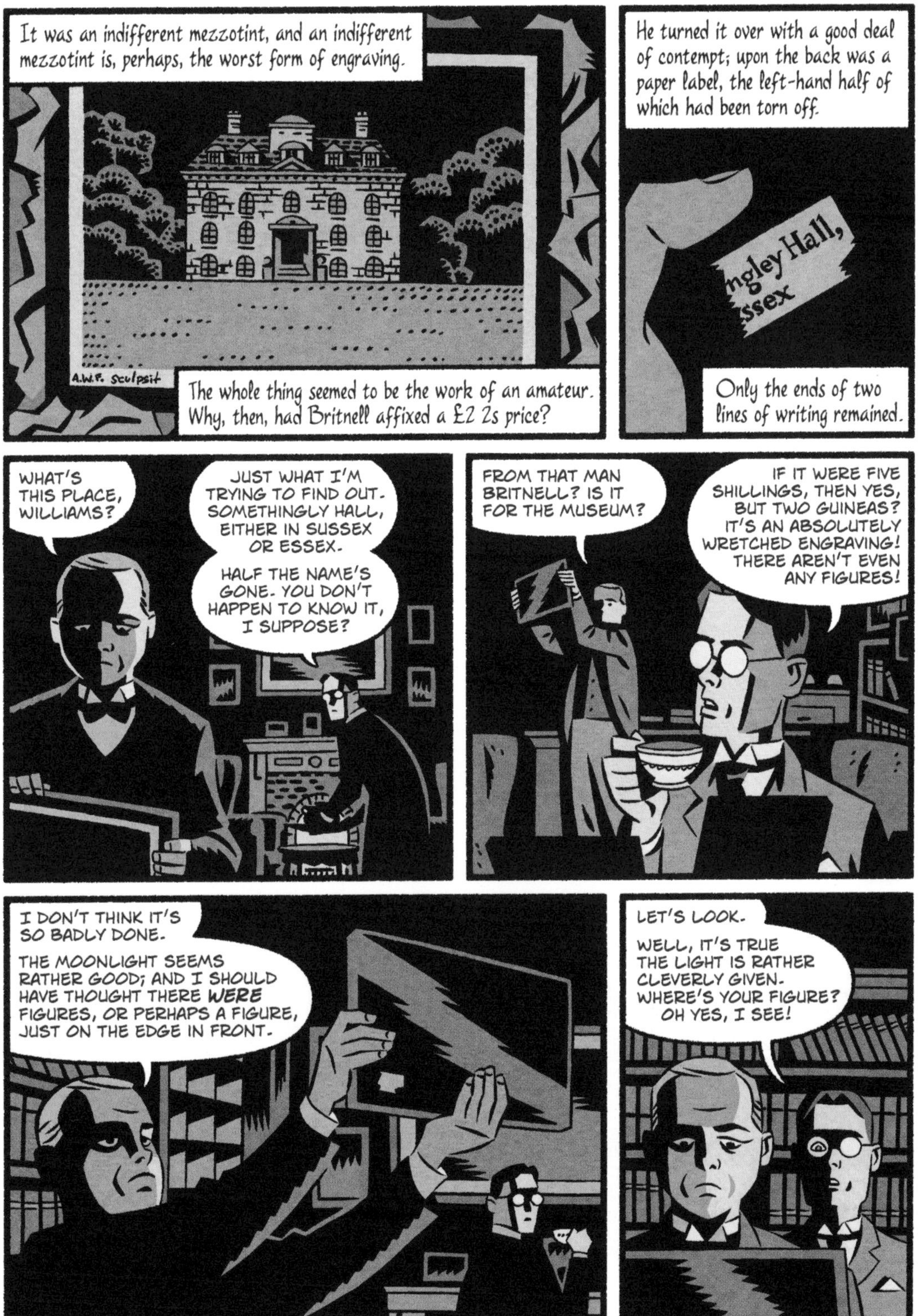
It was an indifferent mezzotint, and an indifferent mezzotint is, perhaps, the worst form of engraving.
A.W.F. sculpsit
The whole thing seemed to be the work of an amateur. Why, then, had Britnell affixed a £2 2s price?
He turned it over with a good deal of contempt; upon the back was a paper label, the left-hand half of which had been torn off.
ngley Hall,
ssex
Only the ends of two lines of writing remained.
WHAT'S THIS PLACE, WILLIAMS?
JUST WHAT I'M TRYING TO FIND OUT. SOMETHINGLY HALL, EITHER IN SUSSEX OR ESSEX.
HALF THE NAME'S GONE. YOU DON'T HAPPEN TO KNOW IT, I SUPPOSE?
FROM THAT MAN BRITNELL? IS IT FOR THE MUSEUM?
IF IT WERE FIVE SHILLINGS, THEN YES, BUT TWO GUINEAS? IT'S AN ABSOLUTELY WRETCHED ENGRAVING! THERE AREN'T EVEN ANY FIGURES!
I DON'T THINK IT'S SO BADLY DONE.
THE MOONLIGHT SEEMS RATHER GOOD; AND I SHOULD HAVE THOUGHT THERE ***WERE*** FIGURES, OR PERHAPS A FIGURE, JUST ON THE EDGE IN FRONT.
LET'S LOOK.
WELL, IT'S TRUE THE LIGHT IS RATHER CLEVERLY GIVEN. WHERE'S YOUR FIGURE? OH YES, I SEE!

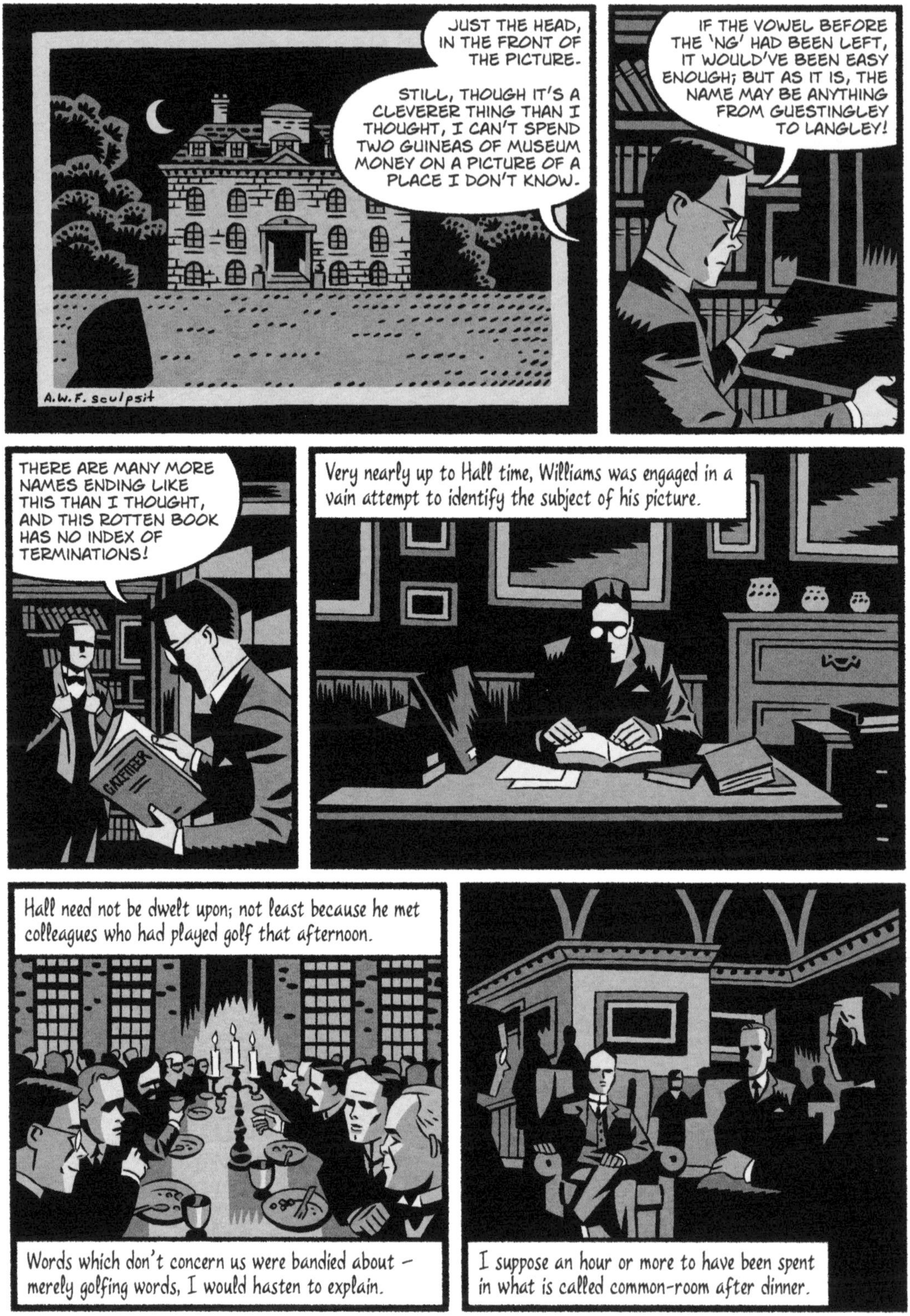
JUST THE HEAD, IN THE FRONT OF THE PICTURE.
STILL, THOUGH IT'S A CLEVERER THING THAN I THOUGHT, I CAN'T SPEND TWO GUINEAS OF MUSEUM MONEY ON A PICTURE OF A PLACE I DON'T KNOW.
A.W.F. sculpsit
IF THE VOWEL BEFORE THE 'NG' HAD BEEN LEFT, IT WOULD'VE BEEN EASY ENOUGH; BUT AS IT IS, THE NAME MAY BE ANYTHING FROM GUESTINGLEY TO LANGLEY!
THERE ARE MANY MORE NAMES ENDING LIKE THIS THAN I THOUGHT, AND THIS ROTTEN BOOK HAS NO INDEX OF TERMINATIONS!
GAZETTEER
Very nearly up to Hall time, Williams was engaged in a vain attempt to identify the subject of his picture.
Hall need not be dwelt upon; not least because he met colleagues who had played golf that afternoon.
Words which don't concern us were bandied about – merely golfing words, I would hasten to explain.
I suppose an hour or more to have been spent in what is called common-room after dinner.

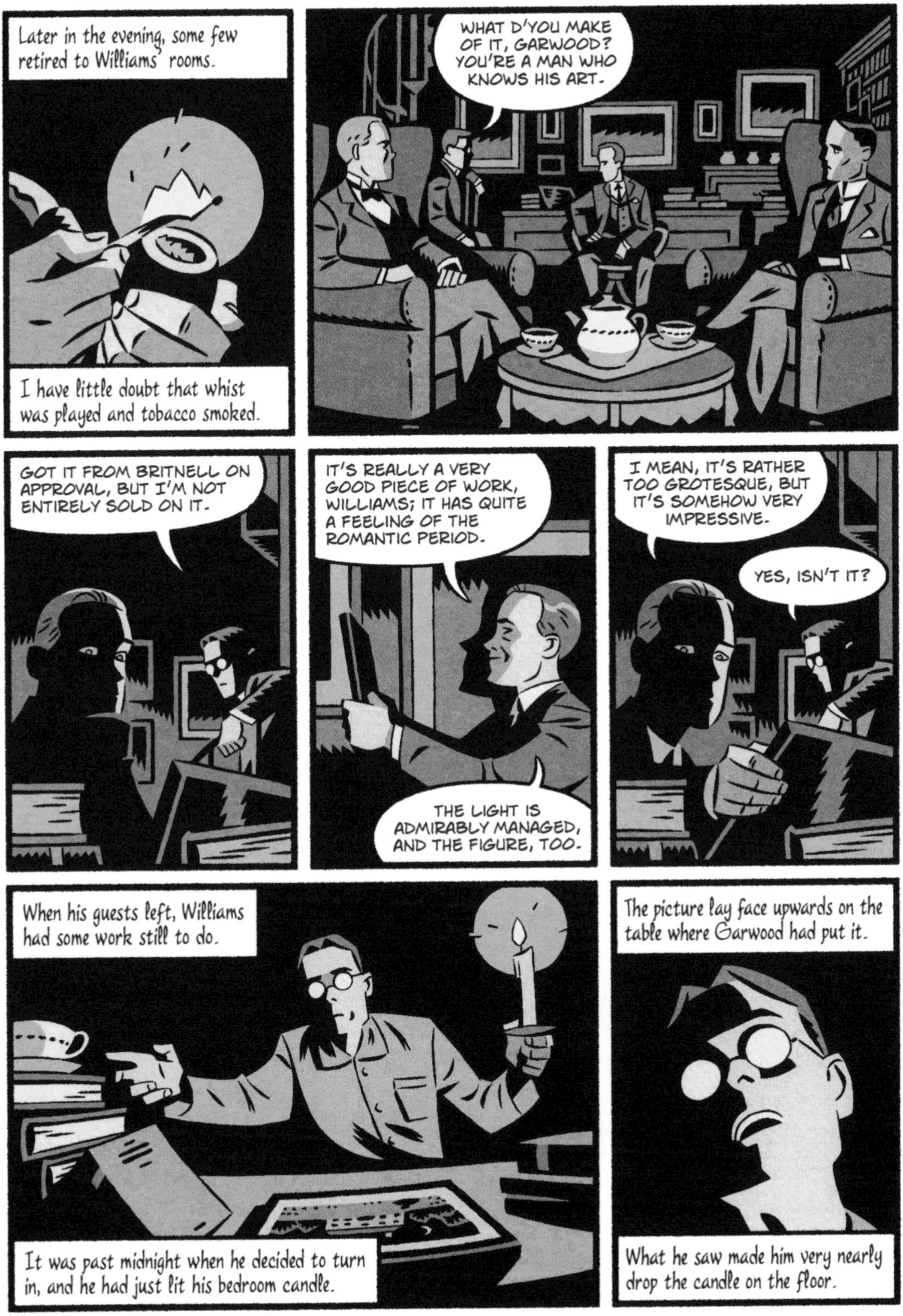
Later in the evening, some few retired to Williams' rooms.
I have little doubt that whist was played and tobacco smoked.
WHAT D'YOU MAKE OF IT, GARWOOD? YOU'RE A MAN WHO KNOWS HIS ART.
GOT IT FROM BRITNELL ON APPROVAL, BUT I'M NOT ENTIRELY SOLD ON IT.
IT'S REALLY A VERY GOOD PIECE OF WORK, WILLIAMS; IT HAS QUITE A FEELING OF THE ROMANTIC PERIOD.
THE LIGHT IS ADMIRABLY MANAGED, AND THE FIGURE, TOO.
I MEAN, IT'S RATHER TOO GROTESQUE, BUT IT'S SOMEHOW VERY IMPRESSIVE.
YES, ISN'T IT?
When his guests left, Williams had some work still to do.
It was past midnight when he decided to turn in, and he had just lit his bedroom candle.
The picture lay face upwards on the table where Garwood had put it.
What he saw made him very nearly drop the candle on the floor.

In the middle of the lawn was a figure where none had been that afternoon. It crawled on all-fours towards the house, muffled in a strange black garment with a white cross on the back.

A.W.F. sculpsit

I do not know what is the ideal course to pursue in a situation of this kind.

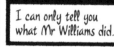

I can only tell you what Mr Williams did.

He took the picture across the passage to some other rooms which he possessed.

There he locked it in a drawer, locked the doors of both sets of rooms and retired for the night.

Before bed, he wrote out and signed an account of the extraordinary change which the picture had undergone since it had come into his possession.

It was consoling to reflect that the picture's behaviour did not only depend upon his unsupported testimony.

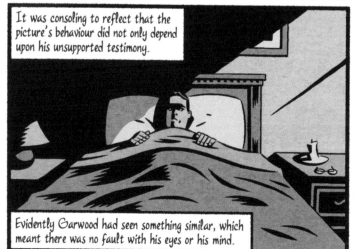

Evidently Garwood had seen something similar, which meant there was no fault with his eyes or his mind.

Tomorrow he must look at the picture very carefully, and get a witness for the purpose — perhaps invite his neighbour Nisbet for breakfast?

He must also discover which house it was that the mezzotint showed.

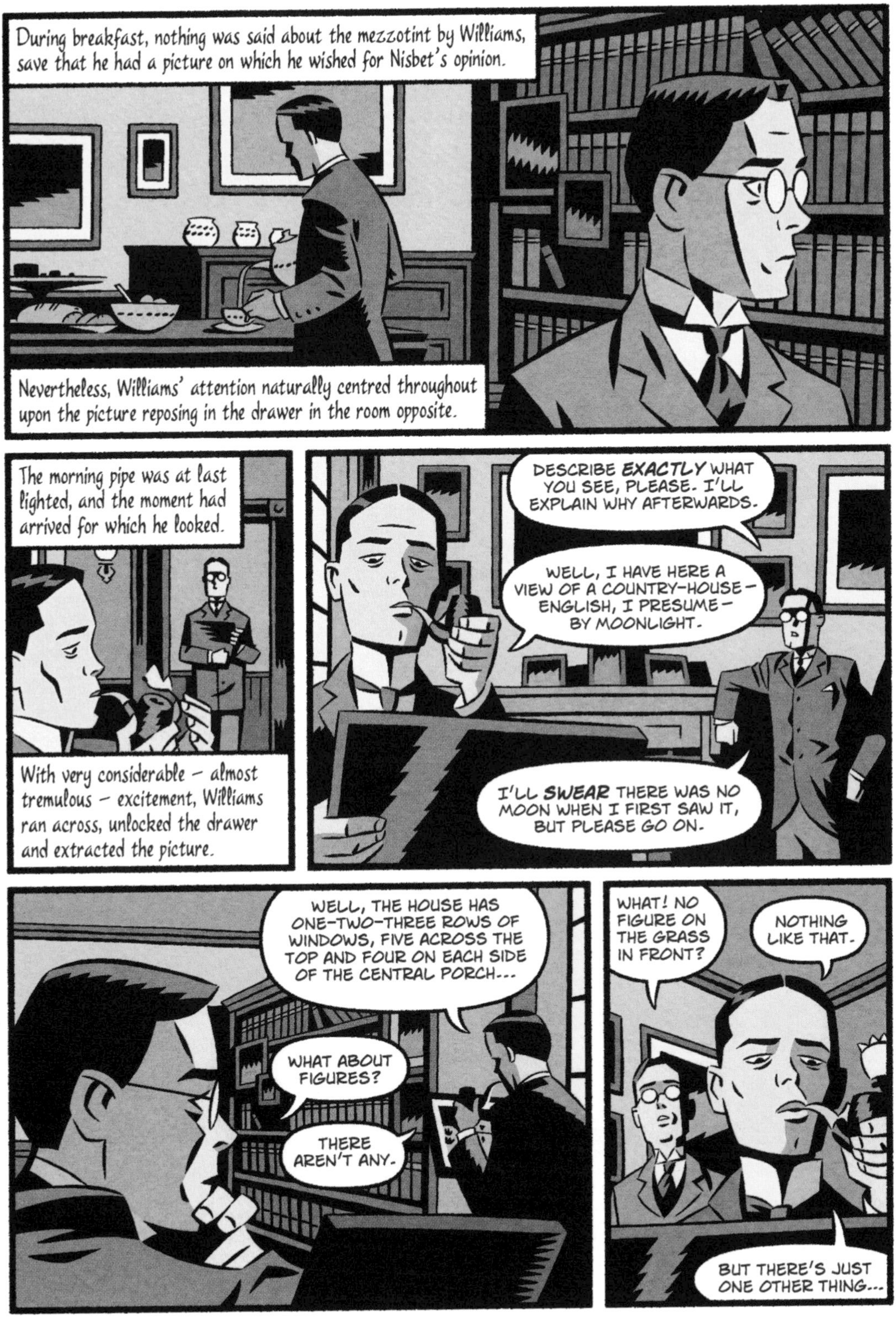
During breakfast, nothing was said about the mezzotint by Williams, save that he had a picture on which he wished for Nisbet's opinion.
Nevertheless, Williams' attention naturally centred throughout upon the picture reposing in the drawer in the room opposite.
The morning pipe was at last lighted, and the moment had arrived for which he looked.
With very considerable – almost tremulous – excitement, Williams ran across, unlocked the drawer and extracted the picture.
DESCRIBE EXACTLY WHAT YOU SEE, PLEASE. I'LL EXPLAIN WHY AFTERWARDS.
WELL, I HAVE HERE A VIEW OF A COUNTRY-HOUSE – ENGLISH, I PRESUME – BY MOONLIGHT.
I'LL SWEAR THERE WAS NO MOON WHEN I FIRST SAW IT, BUT PLEASE GO ON.
WELL, THE HOUSE HAS ONE-TWO-THREE ROWS OF WINDOWS, FIVE ACROSS THE TOP AND FOUR ON EACH SIDE OF THE CENTRAL PORCH...
WHAT ABOUT FIGURES?
THERE AREN'T ANY.
WHAT! NO FIGURE ON THE GRASS IN FRONT?
NOTHING LIKE THAT.
BUT THERE'S JUST ONE OTHER THING...

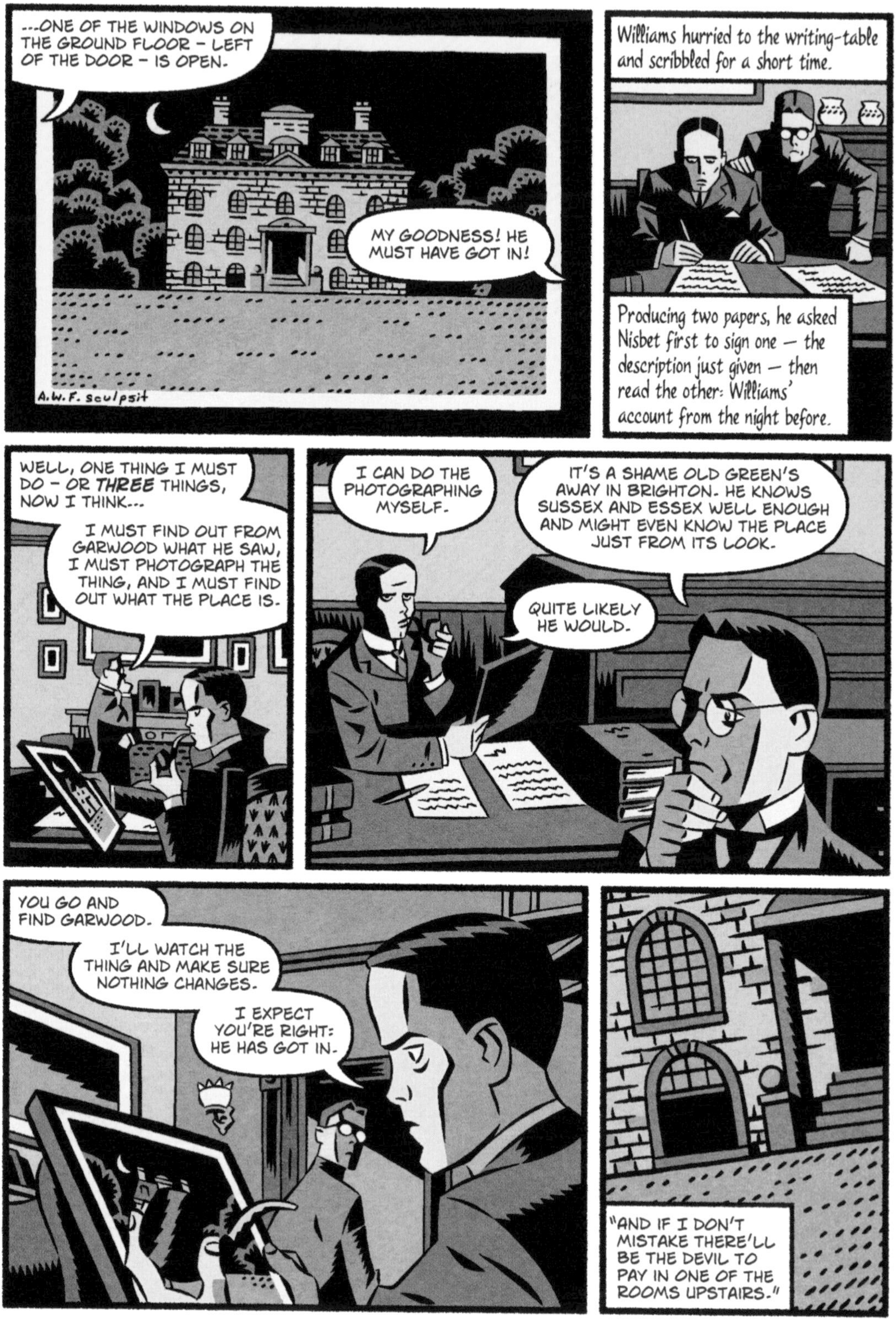

...ONE OF THE WINDOWS ON THE GROUND FLOOR – LEFT OF THE DOOR – IS OPEN.
MY GOODNESS! HE MUST HAVE GOT IN!
A.W.F. sculpsit
Williams hurried to the writing-table and scribbled for a short time.
Producing two papers, he asked Nisbet first to sign one — the description just given — then read the other: Williams' account from the night before.
WELL, ONE THING I MUST DO – OR THREE THINGS, NOW I THINK...
I MUST FIND OUT FROM GARWOOD WHAT HE SAW, I MUST PHOTOGRAPH THE THING, AND I MUST FIND OUT WHAT THE PLACE IS.
I CAN DO THE PHOTOGRAPHING MYSELF.
IT'S A SHAME OLD GREEN'S AWAY IN BRIGHTON. HE KNOWS SUSSEX AND ESSEX WELL ENOUGH AND MIGHT EVEN KNOW THE PLACE JUST FROM ITS LOOK.
QUITE LIKELY HE WOULD.
YOU GO AND FIND GARWOOD.
I'LL WATCH THE THING AND MAKE SURE NOTHING CHANGES.
I EXPECT YOU'RE RIGHT: HE HAS GOT IN.
"AND IF I DON'T MISTAKE THERE'LL BE THE DEVIL TO PAY IN ONE OF THE ROOMS UPSTAIRS."

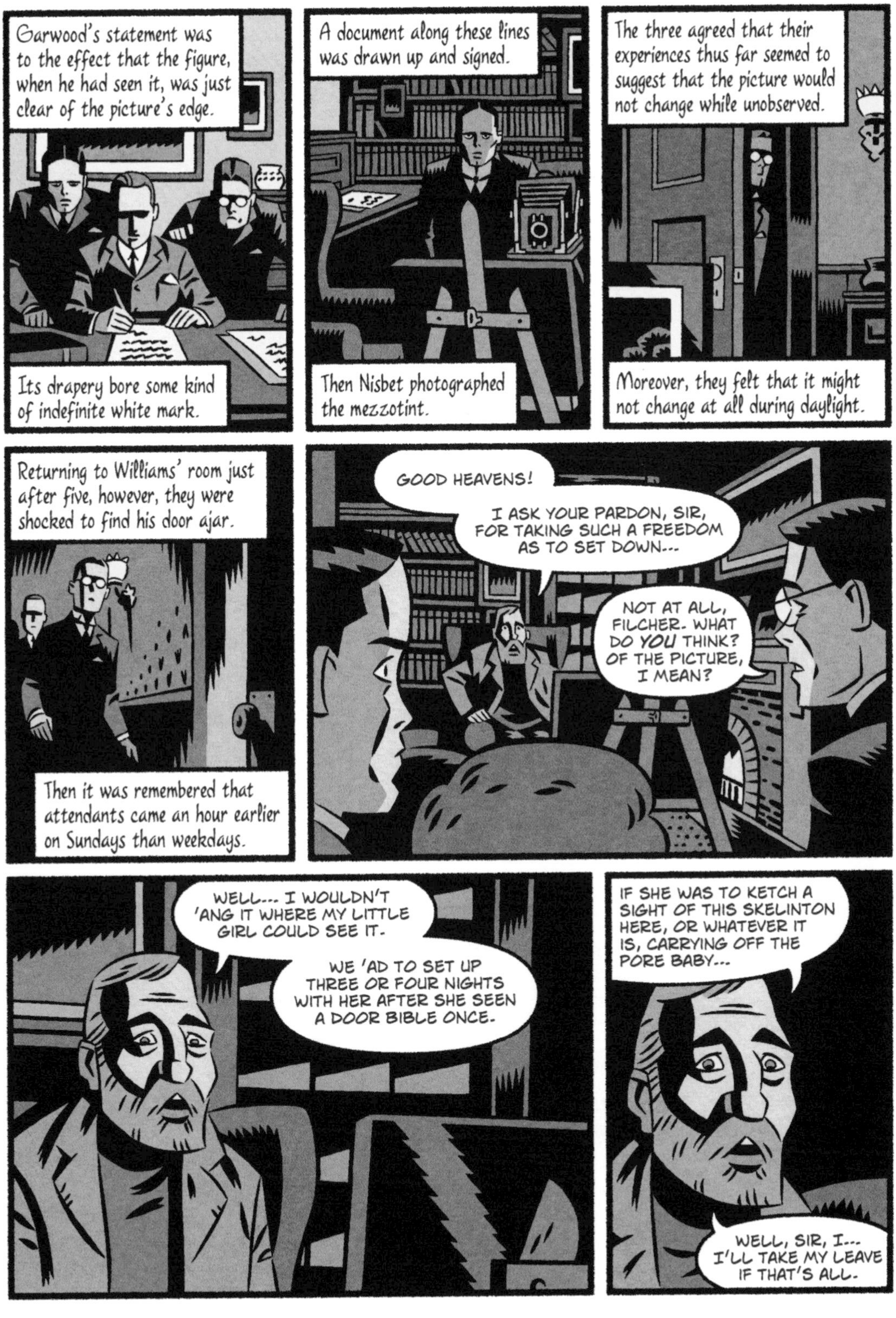
Garwood's statement was to the effect that the figure, when he had seen it, was just clear of the picture's edge.
Its drapery bore some kind of indefinite white mark.
A document along these lines was drawn up and signed.
Then Nisbet photographed the mezzotint.
The three agreed that their experiences thus far seemed to suggest that the picture would not change while unobserved.
Moreover, they felt that it might not change at all during daylight.
Returning to Williams' room just after five, however, they were shocked to find his door ajar.
Then it was remembered that attendants came an hour earlier on Sundays than weekdays.
GOOD HEAVENS!
I ASK YOUR PARDON, SIR, FOR TAKING SUCH A FREEDOM AS TO SET DOWN...
NOT AT ALL, FILCHER. WHAT DO YOU THINK? OF THE PICTURE, I MEAN?
WELL... I WOULDN'T 'ANG IT WHERE MY LITTLE GIRL COULD SEE IT.
WE 'AD TO SET UP THREE OR FOUR NIGHTS WITH HER AFTER SHE SEEN A DOOR BIBLE ONCE.
IF SHE WAS TO KETCH A SIGHT OF THIS SKELINTON HERE, OR WHATEVER IT IS, CARRYING OFF THE PORE BABY...
WELL, SIR, I... I'LL TAKE MY LEAVE IF THAT'S ALL.

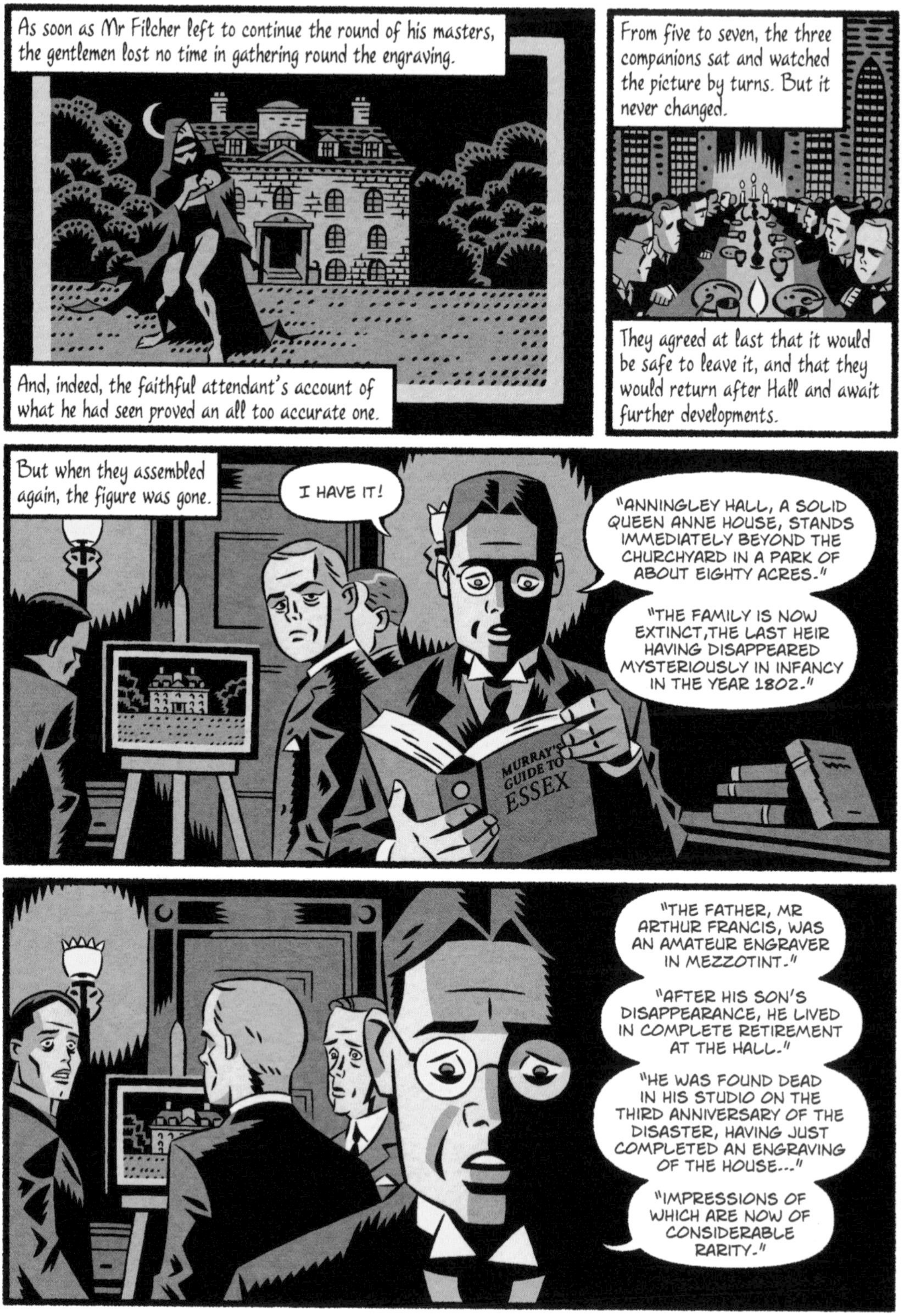
As soon as Mr Filcher left to continue the round of his masters, the gentlemen lost no time in gathering round the engraving.
And, indeed, the faithful attendant's account of what he had seen proved an all too accurate one.
From five to seven, the three companions sat and watched the picture by turns. But it never changed.
They agreed at last that it would be safe to leave it, and that they would return after Hall and await further developments.
But when they assembled again, the figure was gone.
I HAVE IT!
"ANNINGLEY HALL, A SOLID QUEEN ANNE HOUSE, STANDS IMMEDIATELY BEYOND THE CHURCHYARD IN A PARK OF ABOUT EIGHTY ACRES."
"THE FAMILY IS NOW EXTINCT,THE LAST HEIR HAVING DISAPPEARED MYSTERIOUSLY IN INFANCY IN THE YEAR 1802."
MURRAY'S GUIDE TO ESSEX
"THE FATHER, MR ARTHUR FRANCIS, WAS AN AMATEUR ENGRAVER IN MEZZOTINT."
"AFTER HIS SON'S DISAPPEARANCE, HE LIVED IN COMPLETE RETIREMENT AT THE HALL."
"HE WAS FOUND DEAD IN HIS STUDIO ON THE THIRD ANNIVERSARY OF THE DISASTER, HAVING JUST COMPLETED AN ENGRAVING OF THE HOUSE..."
"IMPRESSIONS OF WHICH ARE NOW OF CONSIDERABLE RARITY."

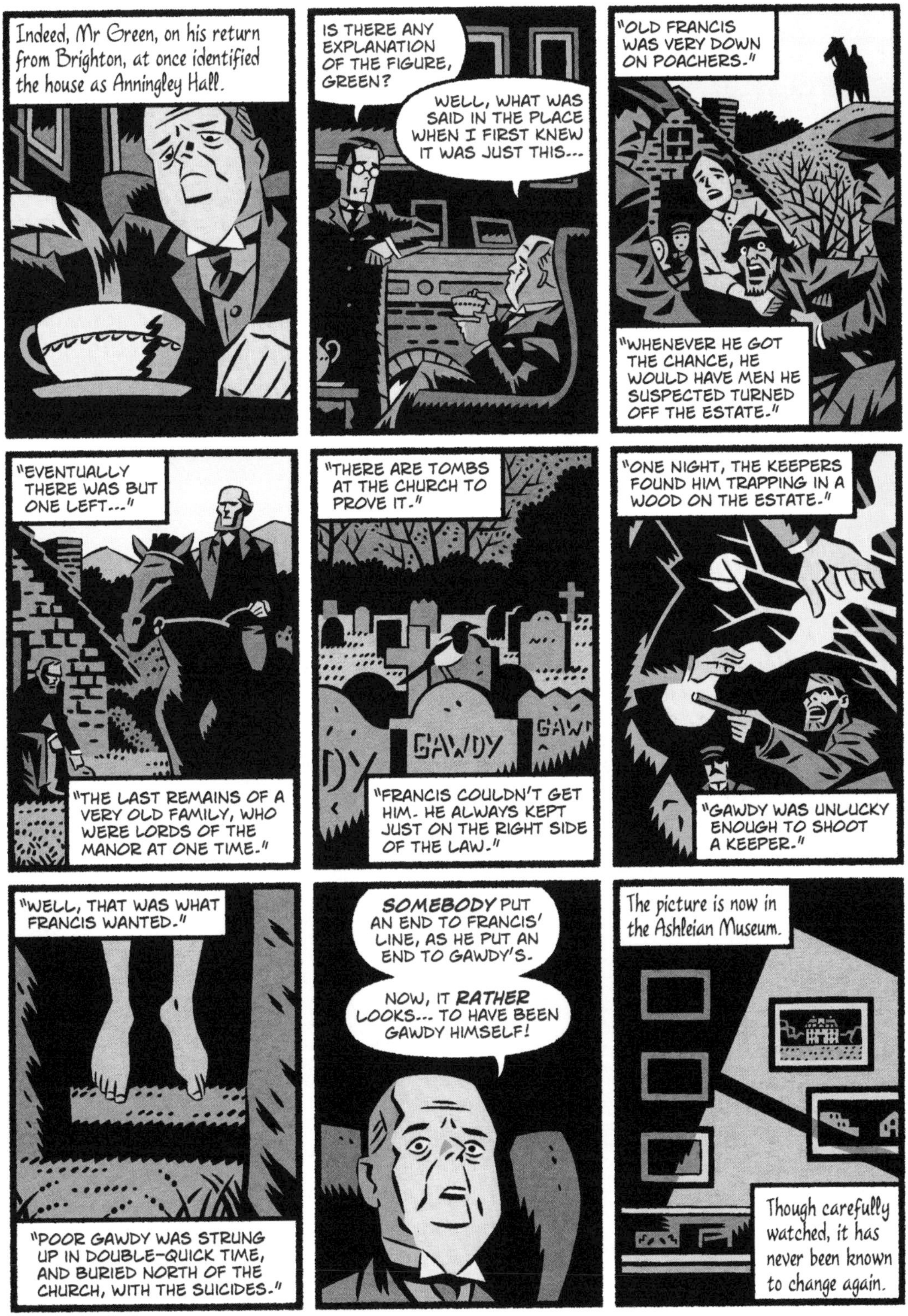
Indeed, Mr Green, on his return from Brighton, at once identified the house as Anningley Hall.
IS THERE ANY EXPLANATION OF THE FIGURE, GREEN?
WELL, WHAT WAS SAID IN THE PLACE WHEN I FIRST KNEW IT WAS JUST THIS...
"OLD FRANCIS WAS VERY DOWN ON POACHERS."
"WHENEVER HE GOT THE CHANCE, HE WOULD HAVE MEN HE SUSPECTED TURNED OFF THE ESTATE."
"EVENTUALLY THERE WAS BUT ONE LEFT..."
"THE LAST REMAINS OF A VERY OLD FAMILY, WHO WERE LORDS OF THE MANOR AT ONE TIME."
"THERE ARE TOMBS AT THE CHURCH TO PROVE IT."
GAWDY
"FRANCIS COULDN'T GET HIM. HE ALWAYS KEPT JUST ON THE RIGHT SIDE OF THE LAW."
"ONE NIGHT, THE KEEPERS FOUND HIM TRAPPING IN A WOOD ON THE ESTATE."
"GAWDY WAS UNLUCKY ENOUGH TO SHOOT A KEEPER."
"WELL, THAT WAS WHAT FRANCIS WANTED."
"POOR GAWDY WAS STRUNG UP IN DOUBLE-QUICK TIME, AND BURIED NORTH OF THE CHURCH, WITH THE SUICIDES."
SOMEBODY PUT AN END TO FRANCIS' LINE, AS HE PUT AN END TO GAWDY'S.
NOW, IT RATHER LOOKS... TO HAVE BEEN GAWDY HIMSELF!
The picture is now in the Ashleian Museum.
Though carefully watched, it has never been known to change again.

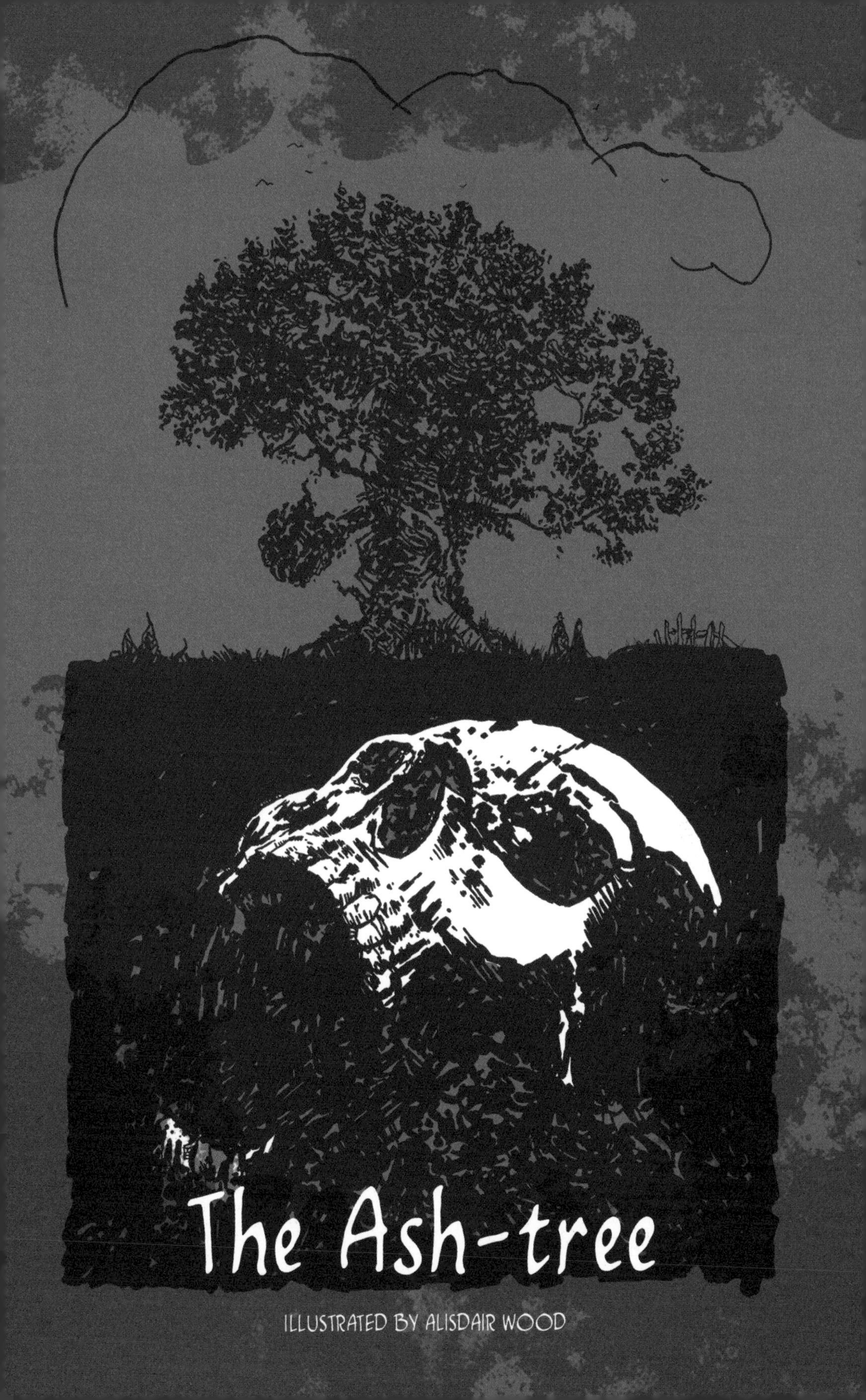
The Ash-tree
ILLUSTRATED BY ALISDAIR WOOD

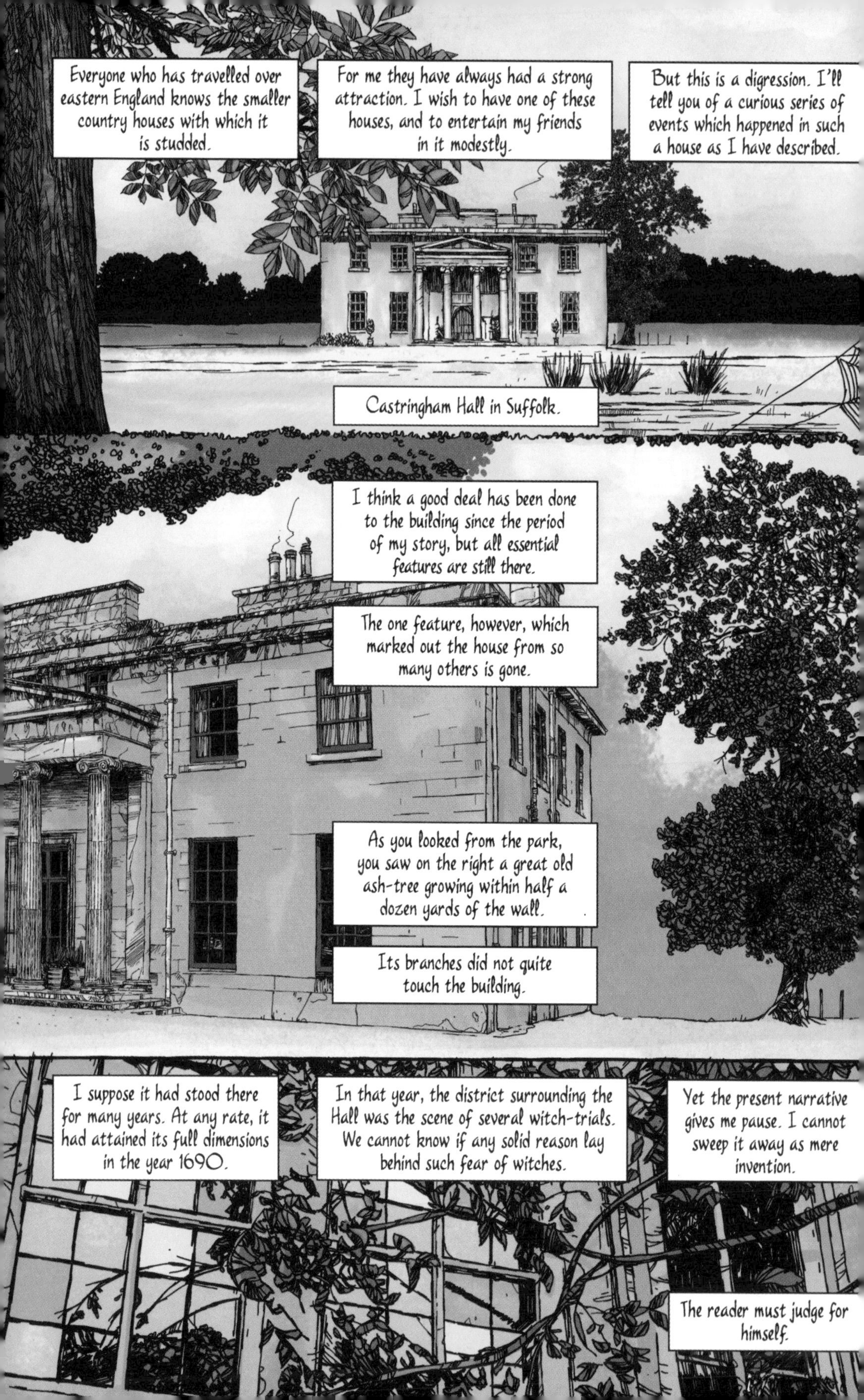
Everyone who has travelled over eastern England knows the smaller country houses with which it is studded.
For me they have always had a strong attraction. I wish to have one of these houses, and to entertain my friends in it modestly.
But this is a digression. I'll tell you of a curious series of events which happened in such a house as I have described.
Castringham Hall in Suffolk.
I think a good deal has been done to the building since the period of my story, but all essential features are still there.
The one feature, however, which marked out the house from so many others is gone.
As you looked from the park, you saw on the right a great old ash-tree growing within half a dozen yards of the wall.
Its branches did not quite touch the building.
I suppose it had stood there for many years. At any rate, it had attained its full dimensions in the year 1690.
In that year, the district surrounding the Hall was the scene of several witch-trials. We cannot know if any solid reason lay behind such fear of witches.
Yet the present narrative gives me pause. I cannot sweep it away as mere invention.
The reader must judge for himself.

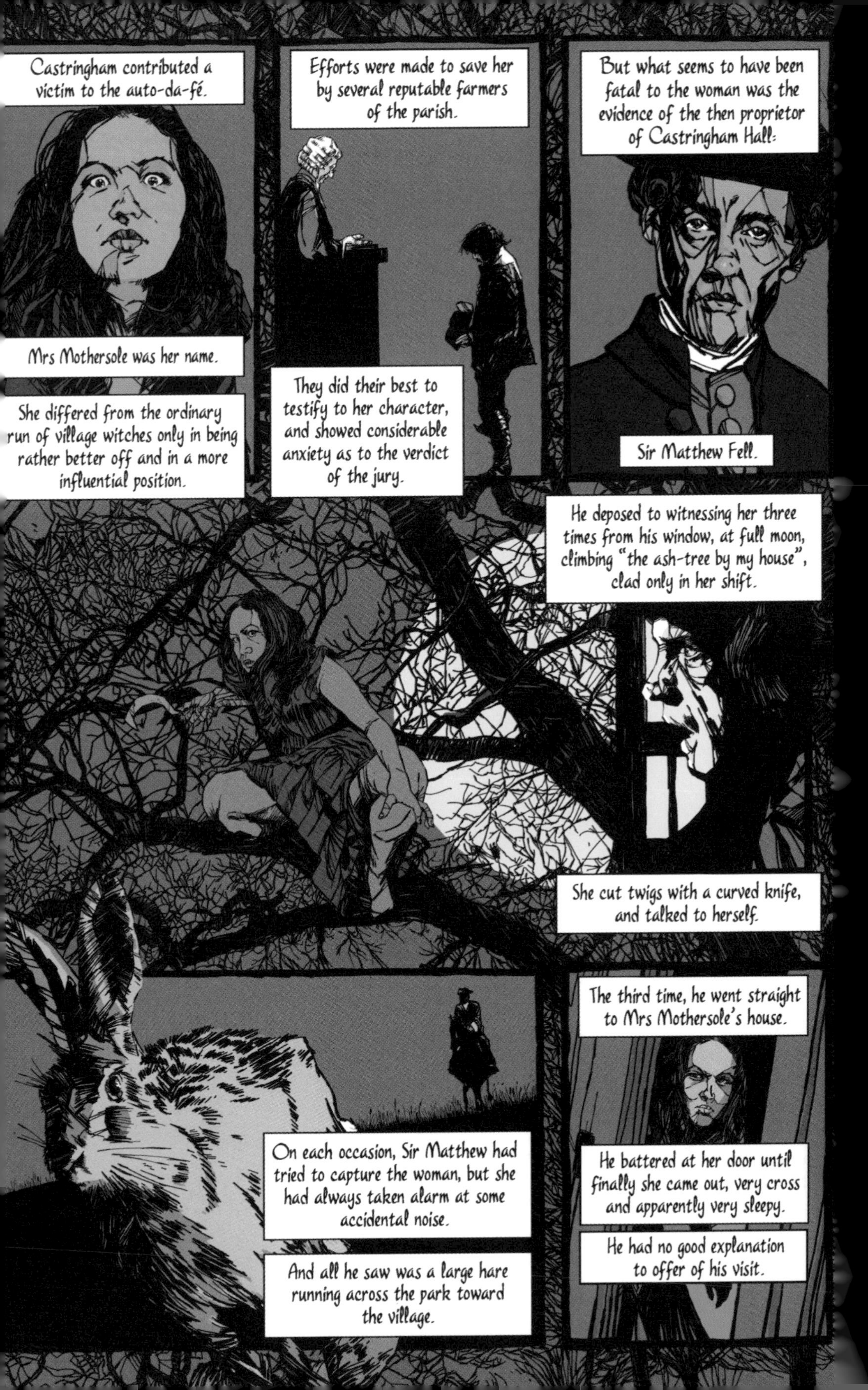
Castringham contributed a victim to the auto-da-fé.
Mrs Mothersole was her name.
She differed from the ordinary run of village witches only in being rather better off and in a more influential position.
Efforts were made to save her by several reputable farmers of the parish.
They did their best to testify to her character, and showed considerable anxiety as to the verdict of the jury.
But what seems to have been fatal to the woman was the evidence of the then proprietor of Castringham Hall:
Sir Matthew Fell.
He deposed to witnessing her three times from his window, at full moon, climbing "the ash-tree by my house", clad only in her shift.
She cut twigs with a curved knife, and talked to herself.
On each occasion, Sir Matthew had tried to capture the woman, but she had always taken alarm at some accidental noise.
And all he saw was a large hare running across the park toward the village.
The third time, he went straight to Mrs Mothersole's house.
He battered at her door until finally she came out, very cross and apparently very sleepy.
He had no good explanation to offer of his visit.

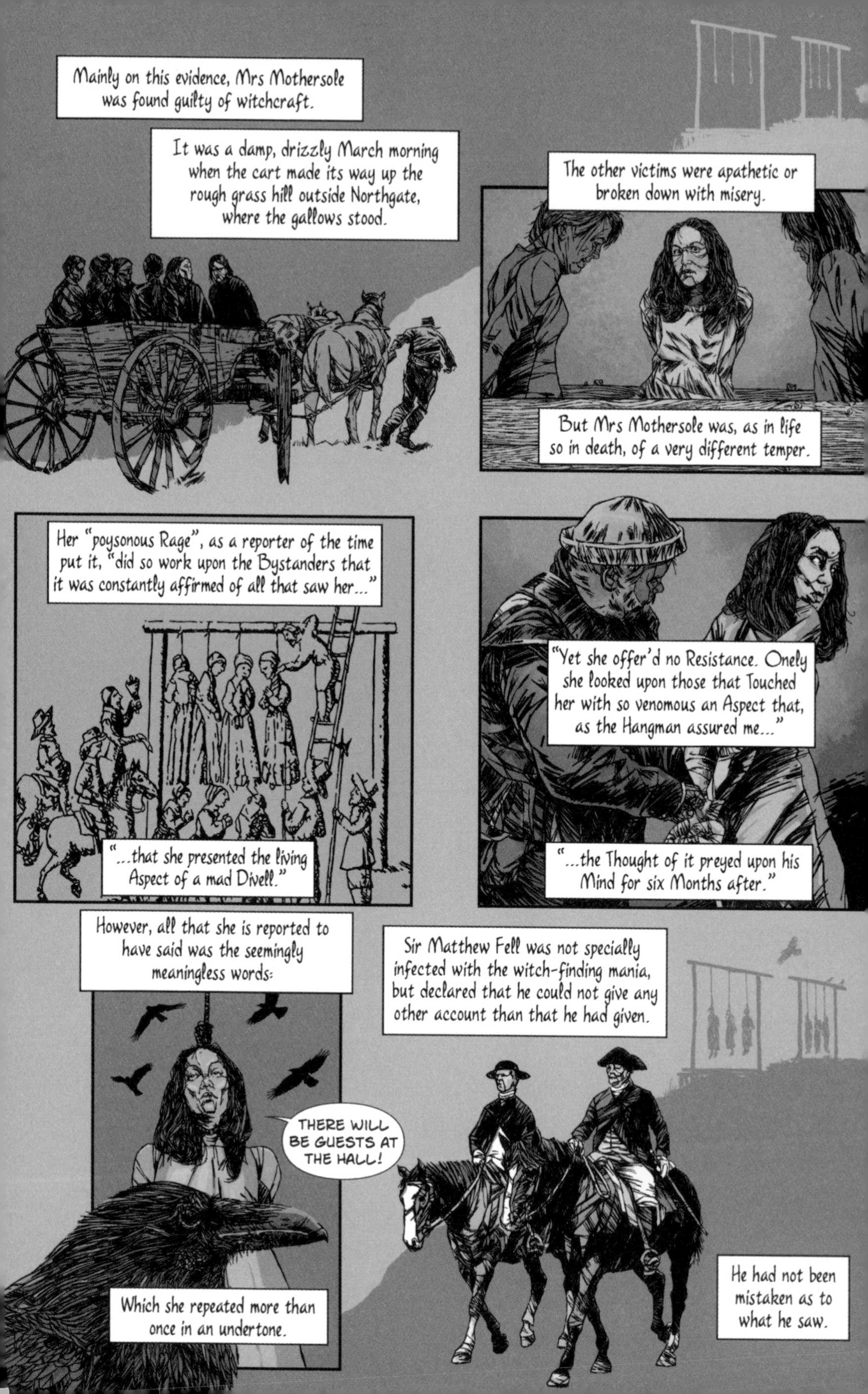
Mainly on this evidence, Mrs Mothersole was found guilty of witchcraft.
It was a damp, drizzly March morning when the cart made its way up the rough grass hill outside Northgate, where the gallows stood.
The other victims were apathetic or broken down with misery.
But Mrs Mothersole was, as in life so in death, of a very different temper.
Her "poysonous Rage", as a reporter of the time put it, "did so work upon the Bystanders that it was constantly affirmed of all that saw her..."
"...that she presented the living Aspect of a mad Divell."
"Yet she offer'd no Resistance. Onely she looked upon those that Touched her with so venomous an Aspect that, as the Hangman assured me..."
"...the Thought of it preyed upon his Mind for six Months after."
However, all that she is reported to have said was the seemingly meaningless words:
THERE WILL BE GUESTS AT THE HALL!
Which she repeated more than once in an undertone.
Sir Matthew Fell was not specially infected with the witch-finding mania, but declared that he could not give any other account than that he had given.
He had not been mistaken as to what he saw.

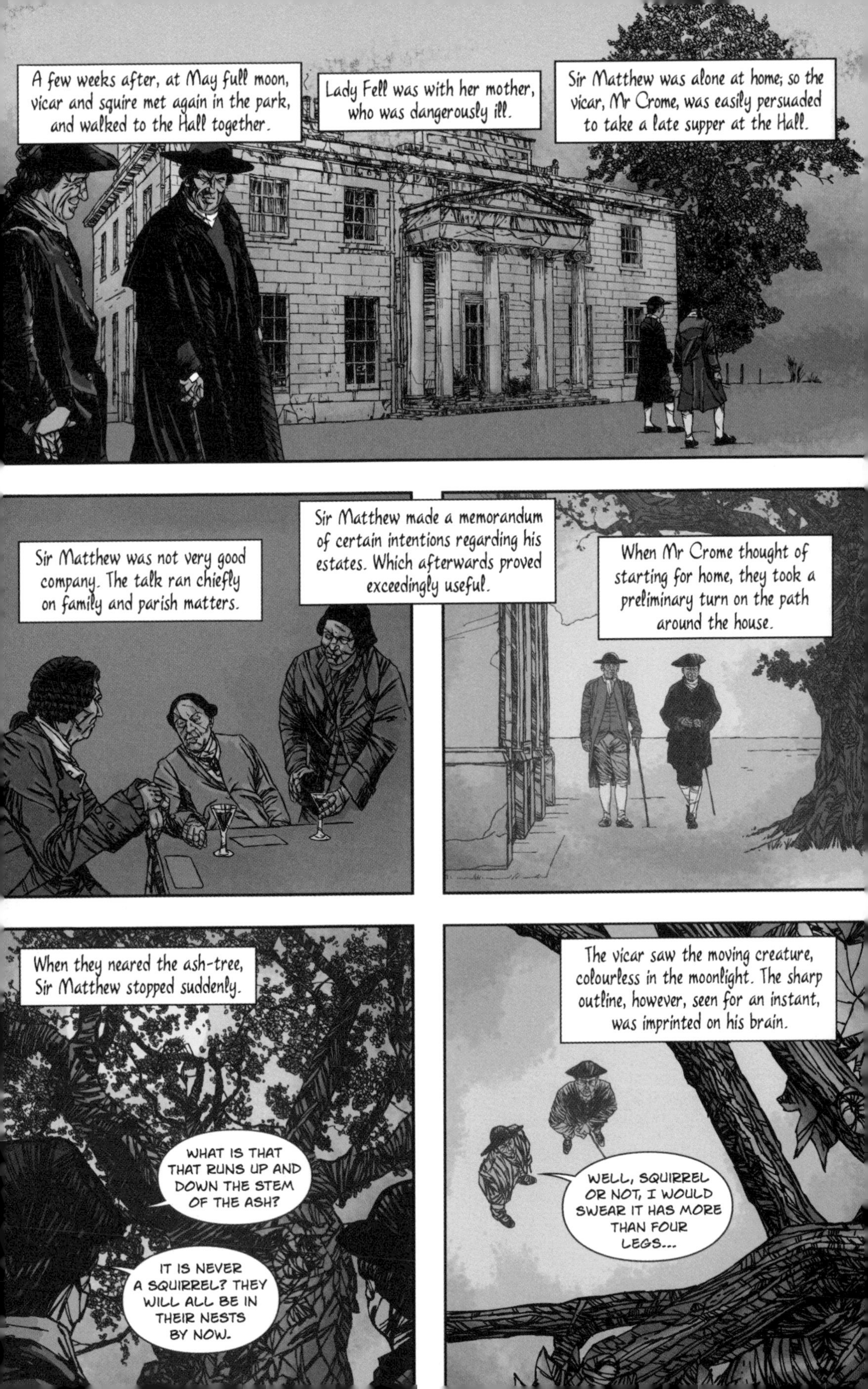
A few weeks after, at May full moon, vicar and squire met again in the park, and walked to the Hall together.
Lady Fell was with her mother, who was dangerously ill.
Sir Matthew was alone at home; so the vicar, Mr Crome, was easily persuaded to take a late supper at the Hall.
Sir Matthew was not very good company. The talk ran chiefly on family and parish matters.
Sir Matthew made a memorandum of certain intentions regarding his estates. Which afterwards proved exceedingly useful.
When Mr Crome thought of starting for home, they took a preliminary turn on the path around the house.
When they neared the ash-tree, Sir Matthew stopped suddenly.
WHAT IS THAT THAT RUNS UP AND DOWN THE STEM OF THE ASH?
IT IS NEVER A SQUIRREL? THEY WILL ALL BE IN THEIR NESTS BY NOW.
The vicar saw the moving creature, colourless in the moonlight. The sharp outline, however, seen for an instant, was imprinted on his brain.
WELL, SQUIRREL OR NOT, I WOULD SWEAR IT HAS MORE THAN FOUR LEGS...

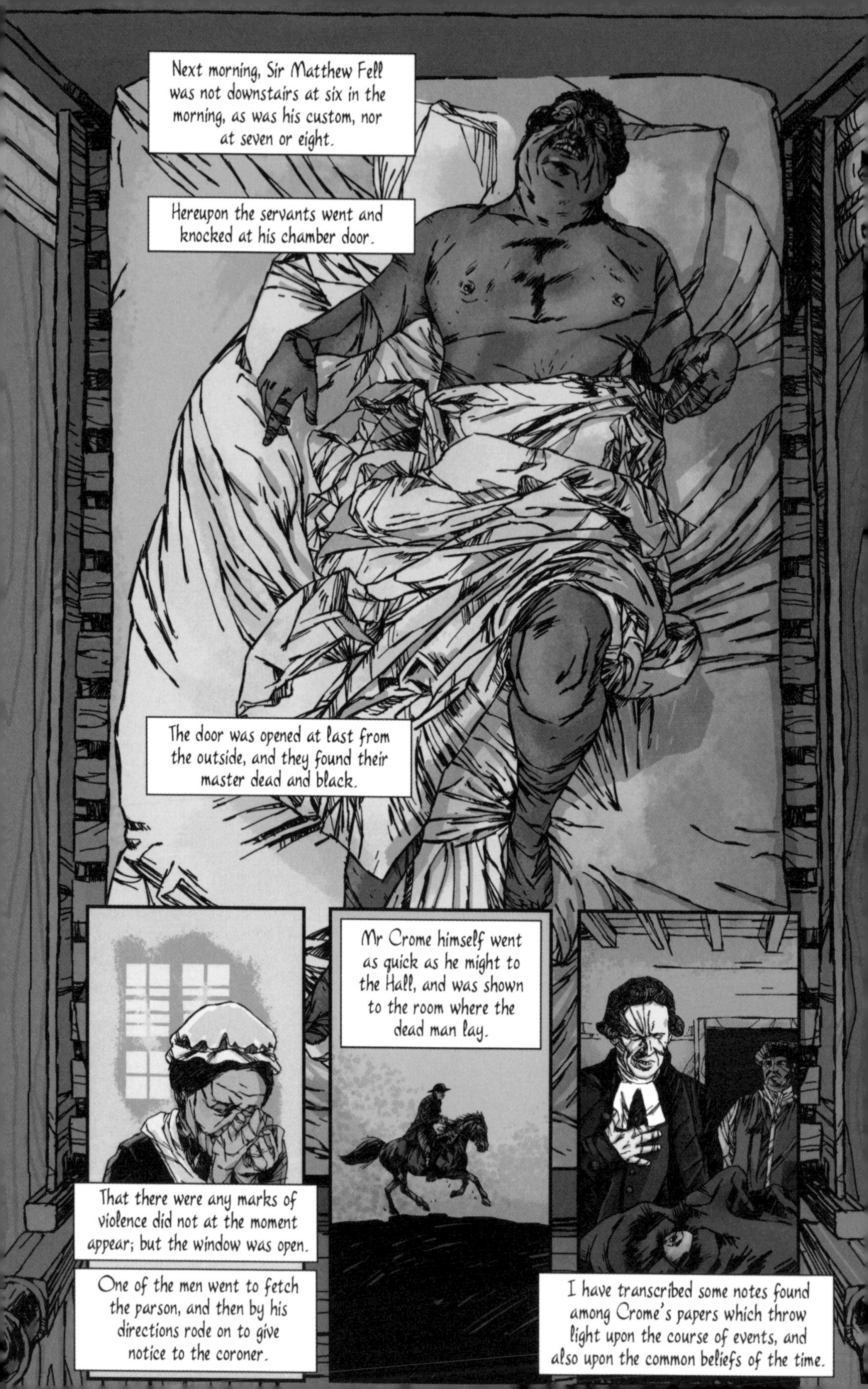
Next morning, Sir Matthew Fell was not downstairs at six in the morning, as was his custom, nor at seven or eight.
Hereupon the servants went and knocked at his chamber door.
The door was opened at last from the outside, and they found their master dead and black.
That there were any marks of violence did not at the moment appear; but the window was open.
One of the men went to fetch the parson, and then by his directions rode on to give notice to the coroner.
Mr Crome himself went as quick as he might to the Hall, and was shown to the room where the dead man lay.
I have transcribed some notes found among Crome's papers which throw light upon the course of events, and also upon the common beliefs of the time.

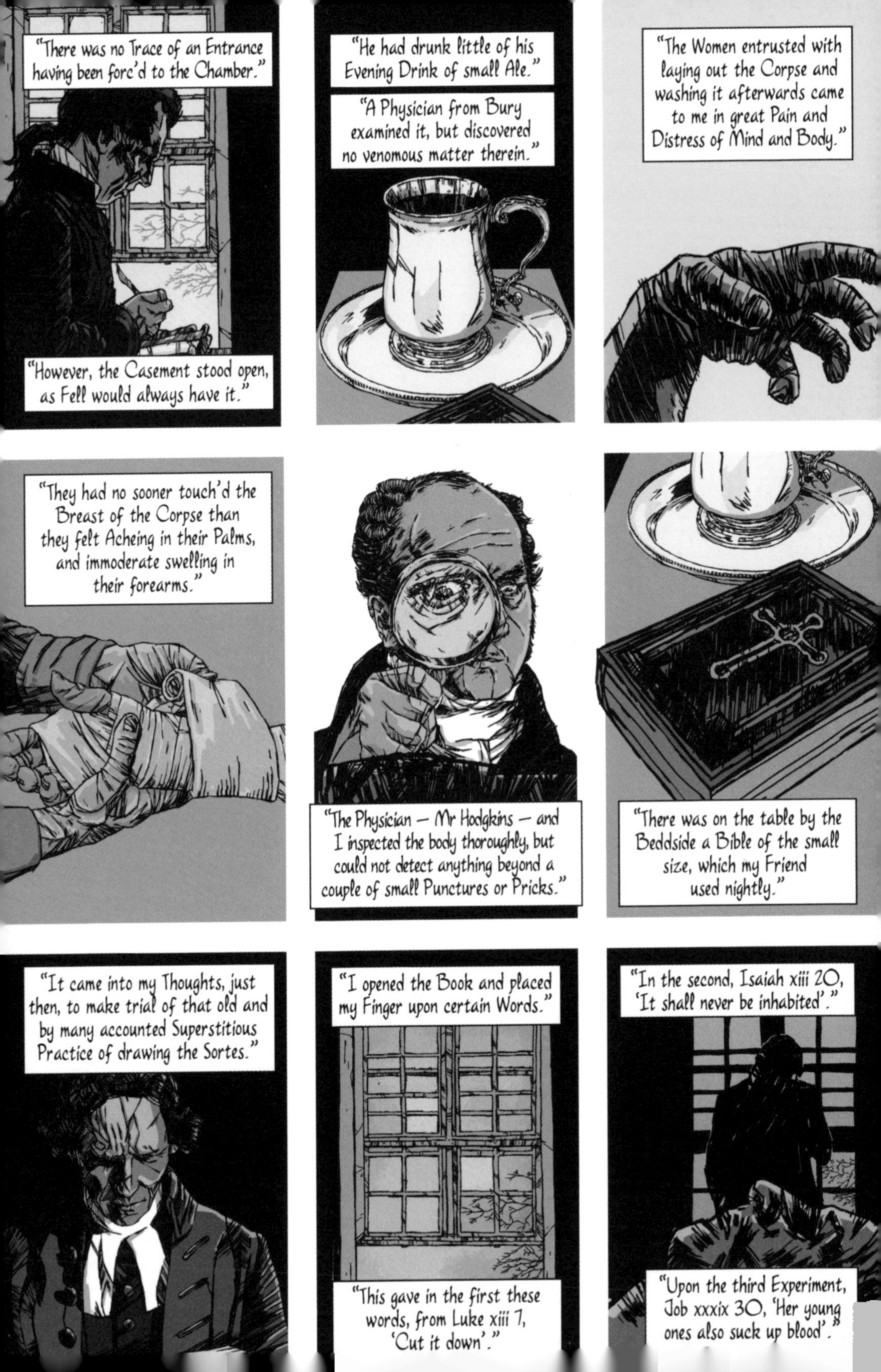
"There was no Trace of an Entrance having been forc'd to the Chamber."
"However, the Casement stood open, as Fell would always have it."
"He had drunk little of his Evening Drink of small Ale."
"A Physician from Bury examined it, but discovered no venomous matter therein."
"The Women entrusted with laying out the Corpse and washing it afterwards came to me in great Pain and Distress of Mind and Body."
"They had no sooner touch'd the Breast of the Corpse than they felt Acheing in their Palms, and immoderate swelling in their forearms."
"The Physician — Mr Hodgkins — and I inspected the body thoroughly, but could not detect anything beyond a couple of small Punctures or Pricks."
"There was on the table by the Beddside a Bible of the small size, which my Friend used nightly."
"It came into my Thoughts, just then, to make trial of that old and by many accounted Superstitious Practice of drawing the Sortes."
"I opened the Book and placed my Finger upon certain Words."
"This gave in the first these words, from Luke xiii 7, 'Cut it down'."
"In the second, Isaiah xiii 20, 'It shall never be inhabited'."
"Upon the third Experiment, Job xxxix 30, 'Her young ones also suck up blood'."

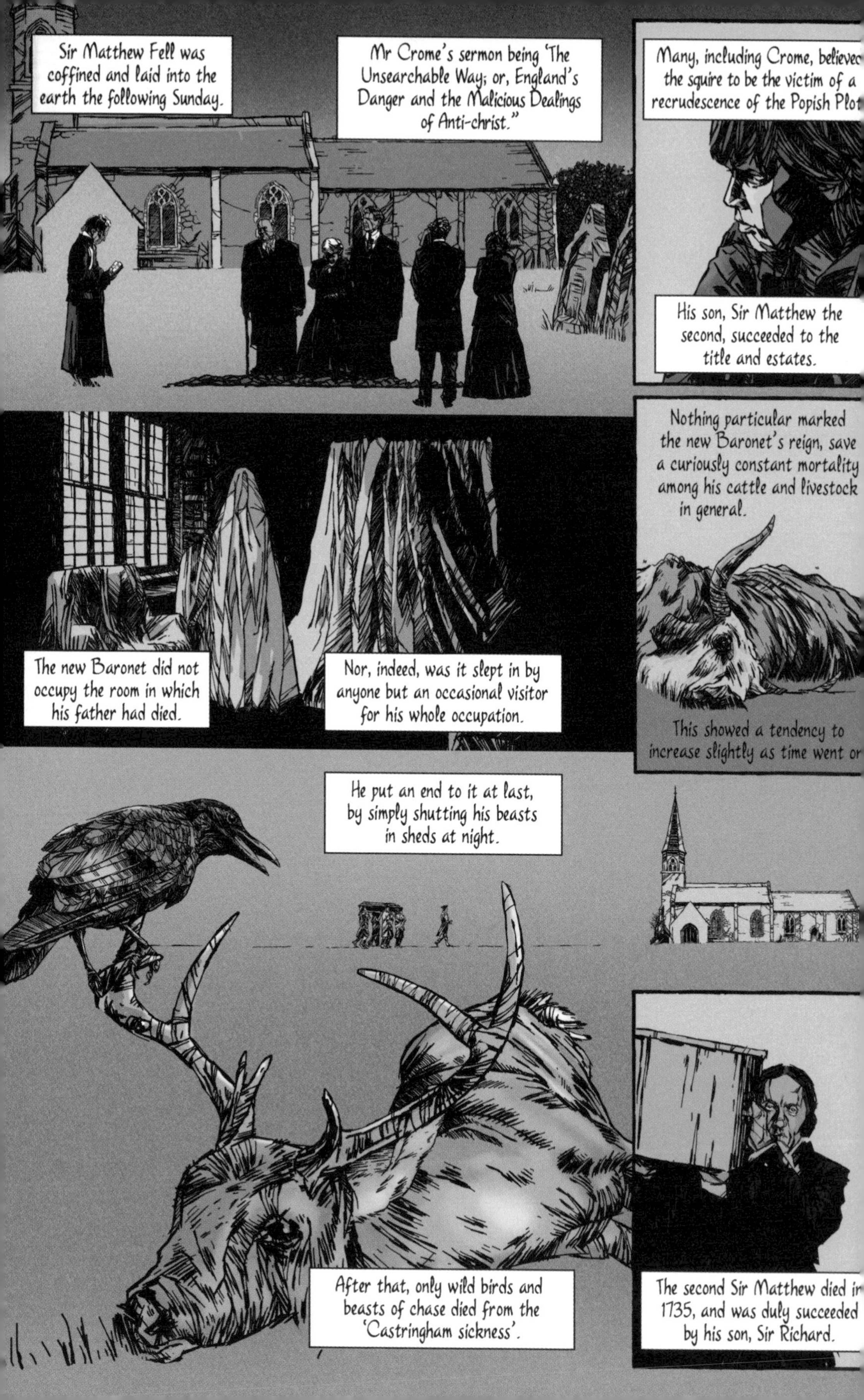
Sir Matthew Fell was coffined and laid into the earth the following Sunday.
Mr Crome's sermon being 'The Unsearchable Way; or, England's Danger and the Malicious Dealings of Anti-christ."
Many, including Crome, believed the squire to be the victim of a recrudescence of the Popish Plot
His son, Sir Matthew the second, succeeded to the title and estates.
The new Baronet did not occupy the room in which his father had died.
Nor, indeed, was it slept in by anyone but an occasional visitor for his whole occupation.
Nothing particular marked the new Baronet's reign, save a curiously constant mortality among his cattle and livestock in general.
This showed a tendency to increase slightly as time went on
He put an end to it at last, by simply shutting his beasts in sheds at night.
After that, only wild birds and beasts of chase died from the 'Castringham sickness'.
The second Sir Matthew died in 1735, and was duly succeeded by his son, Sir Richard.

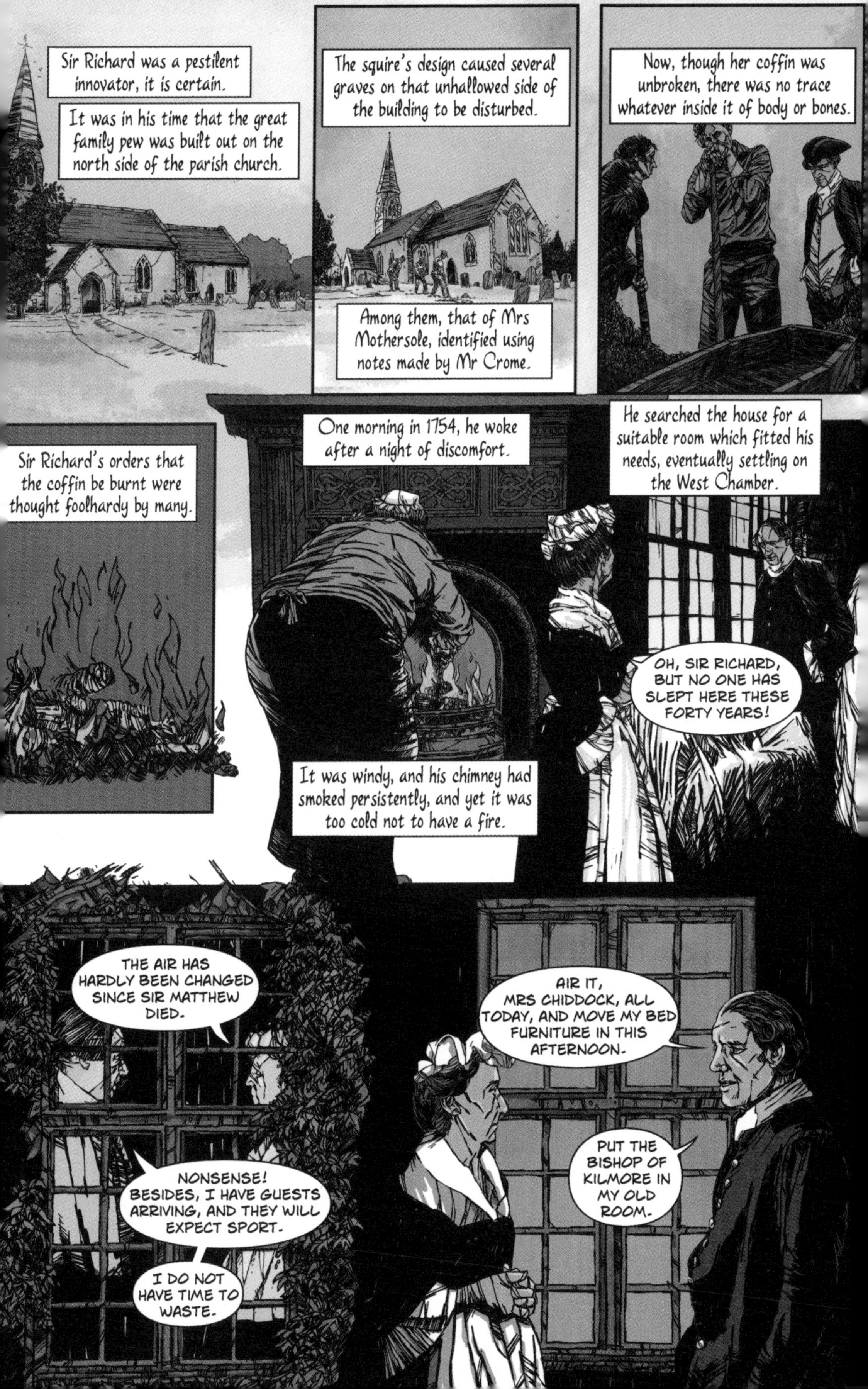
Sir Richard was a pestilent innovator, it is certain.
It was in his time that the great family pew was built out on the north side of the parish church.
The squire's design caused several graves on that unhallowed side of the building to be disturbed.
Among them, that of Mrs Mothersole, identified using notes made by Mr Crome.
Now, though her coffin was unbroken, there was no trace whatever inside it of body or bones.
Sir Richard's orders that the coffin be burnt were thought foolhardy by many.
One morning in 1754, he woke after a night of discomfort.
It was windy, and his chimney had smoked persistently, and yet it was too cold not to have a fire.
He searched the house for a suitable room which fitted his needs, eventually settling on the West Chamber.
OH, SIR RICHARD, BUT NO ONE HAS SLEPT HERE THESE FORTY YEARS!
THE AIR HAS HARDLY BEEN CHANGED SINCE SIR MATTHEW DIED.
NONSENSE! BESIDES, I HAVE GUESTS ARRIVING, AND THEY WILL EXPECT SPORT.
I DO NOT HAVE TIME TO WASTE.
AIR IT, MRS CHIDDOCK, ALL TODAY, AND MOVE MY BED FURNITURE IN THIS AFTERNOON.
PUT THE BISHOP OF KILMORE IN MY OLD ROOM.

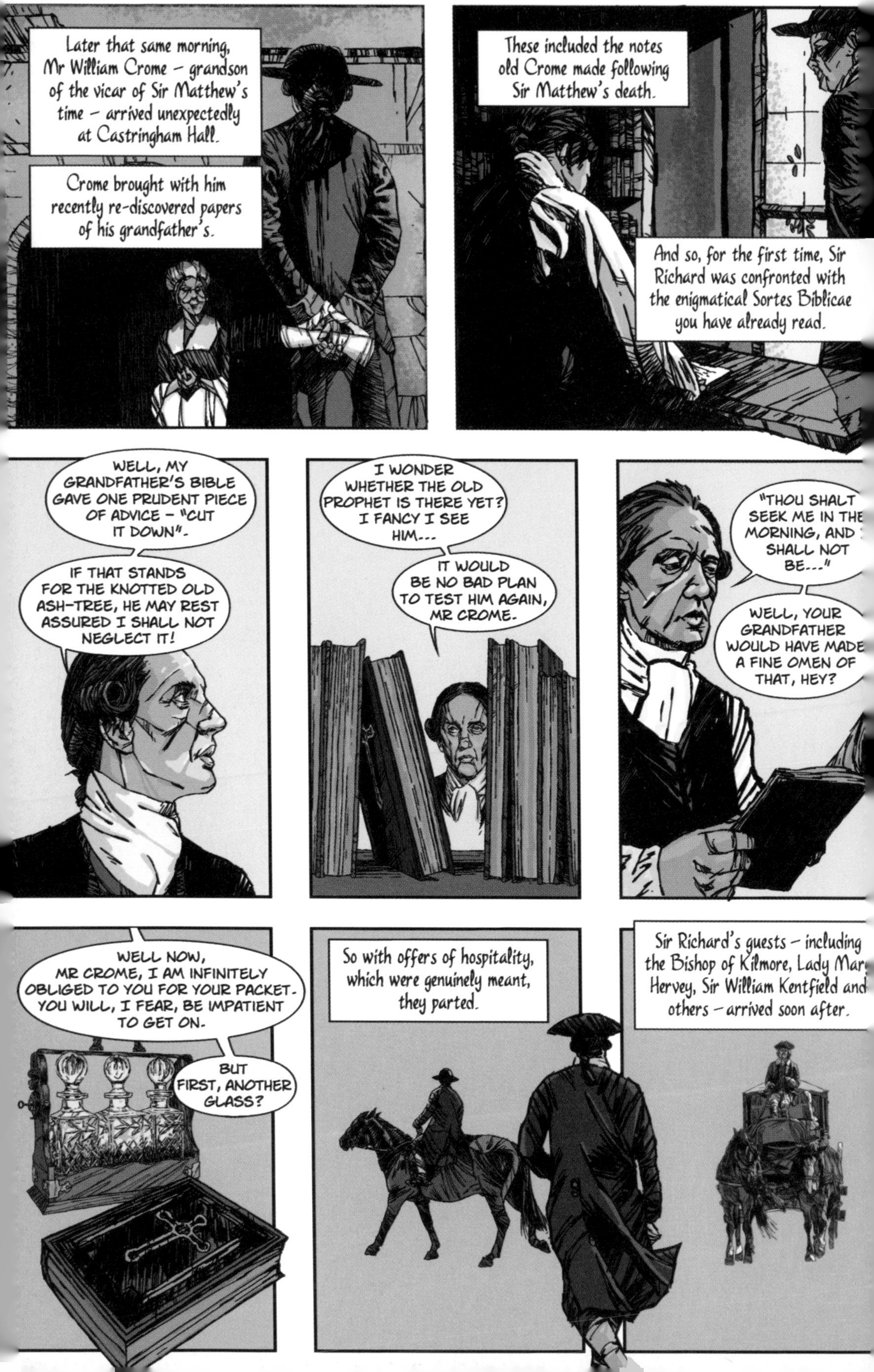
Later that same morning, Mr William Crome – grandson of the vicar of Sir Matthew's time – arrived unexpectedly at Castringham Hall.
Crome brought with him recently re-discovered papers of his grandfather's.
These included the notes old Crome made following Sir Matthew's death.
And so, for the first time, Sir Richard was confronted with the enigmatical Sortes Biblicae you have already read.
WELL, MY GRANDFATHER'S BIBLE GAVE ONE PRUDENT PIECE OF ADVICE – "CUT IT DOWN".
IF THAT STANDS FOR THE KNOTTED OLD ASH-TREE, HE MAY REST ASSURED I SHALL NOT NEGLECT IT!
I WONDER WHETHER THE OLD PROPHET IS THERE YET? I FANCY I SEE HIM...
IT WOULD BE NO BAD PLAN TO TEST HIM AGAIN, MR CROME.
"THOU SHALT SEEK ME IN THE MORNING, AND SHALL NOT BE..."
WELL, YOUR GRANDFATHER WOULD HAVE MADE A FINE OMEN OF THAT, HEY?
WELL NOW, MR CROME, I AM INFINITELY OBLIGED TO YOU FOR YOUR PACKET. YOU WILL, I FEAR, BE IMPATIENT TO GET ON.
BUT FIRST, ANOTHER GLASS?
So with offers of hospitality, which were genuinely meant, they parted.
Sir Richard's guests – including the Bishop of Kilmore, Lady Mar Hervey, Sir William Kentfield and others – arrived soon after.

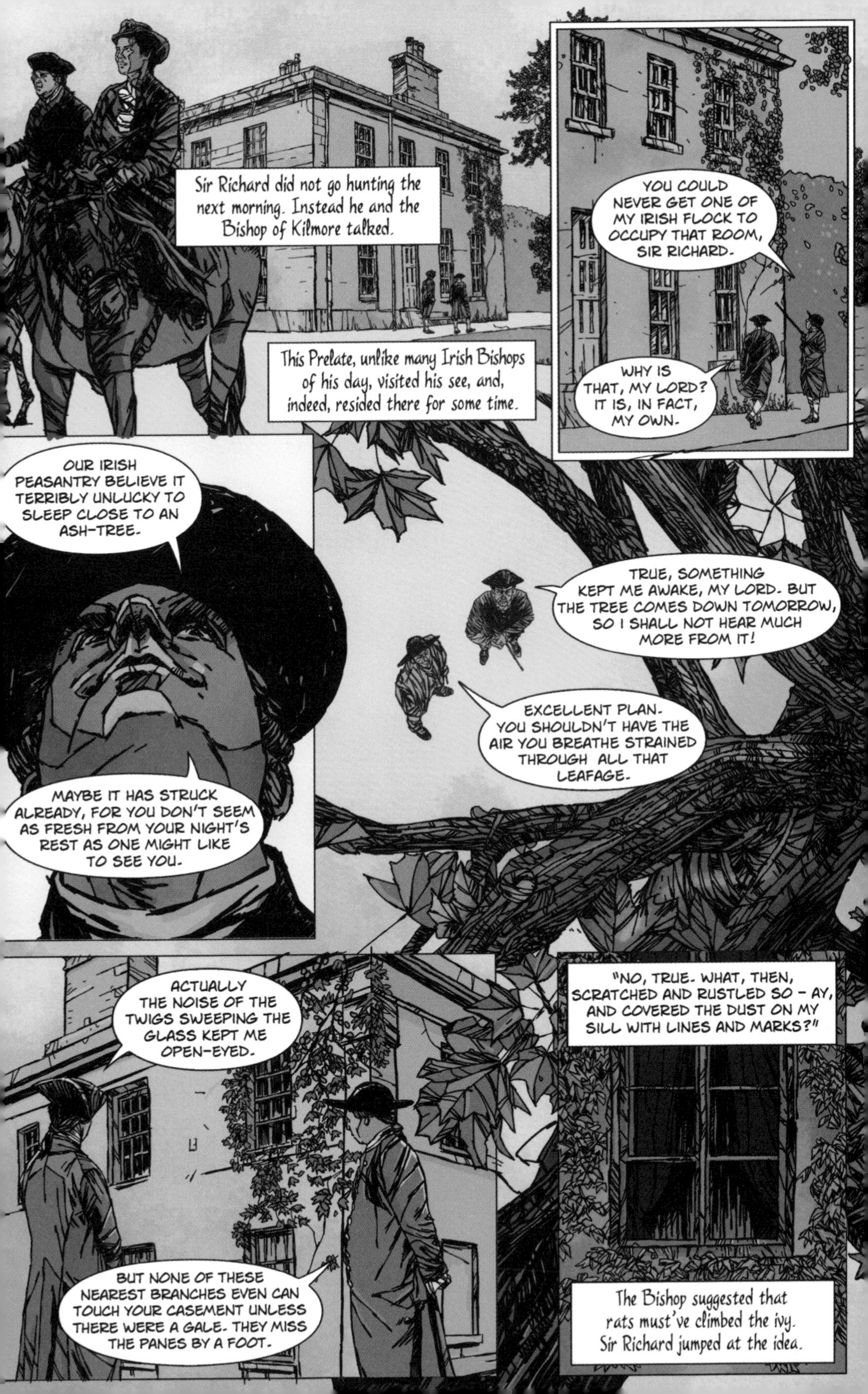
Sir Richard did not go hunting the next morning. Instead he and the Bishop of Kilmore talked.
This Prelate, unlike many Irish Bishops of his day, visited his see, and, indeed, resided there for some time.
YOU COULD NEVER GET ONE OF MY IRISH FLOCK TO OCCUPY THAT ROOM, SIR RICHARD.
WHY IS THAT, MY LORD? IT IS, IN FACT, MY OWN.
OUR IRISH PEASANTRY BELIEVE IT TERRIBLY UNLUCKY TO SLEEP CLOSE TO AN ASH-TREE.
MAYBE IT HAS STRUCK ALREADY, FOR YOU DON'T SEEM AS FRESH FROM YOUR NIGHT'S REST AS ONE MIGHT LIKE TO SEE YOU.
TRUE, SOMETHING KEPT ME AWAKE, MY LORD. BUT THE TREE COMES DOWN TOMORROW, SO I SHALL NOT HEAR MUCH MORE FROM IT!
EXCELLENT PLAN. YOU SHOULDN'T HAVE THE AIR YOU BREATHE STRAINED THROUGH ALL THAT LEAFAGE.
ACTUALLY THE NOISE OF THE TWIGS SWEEPING THE GLASS KEPT ME OPEN-EYED.
BUT NONE OF THESE NEAREST BRANCHES EVEN CAN TOUCH YOUR CASEMENT UNLESS THERE WERE A GALE. THEY MISS THE PANES BY A FOOT.
"NO, TRUE. WHAT, THEN, SCRATCHED AND RUSTLED SO – AY, AND COVERED THE DUST ON MY SILL WITH LINES AND MARKS?"
The Bishop suggested that rats must've climbed the ivy. Sir Richard jumped at the idea.

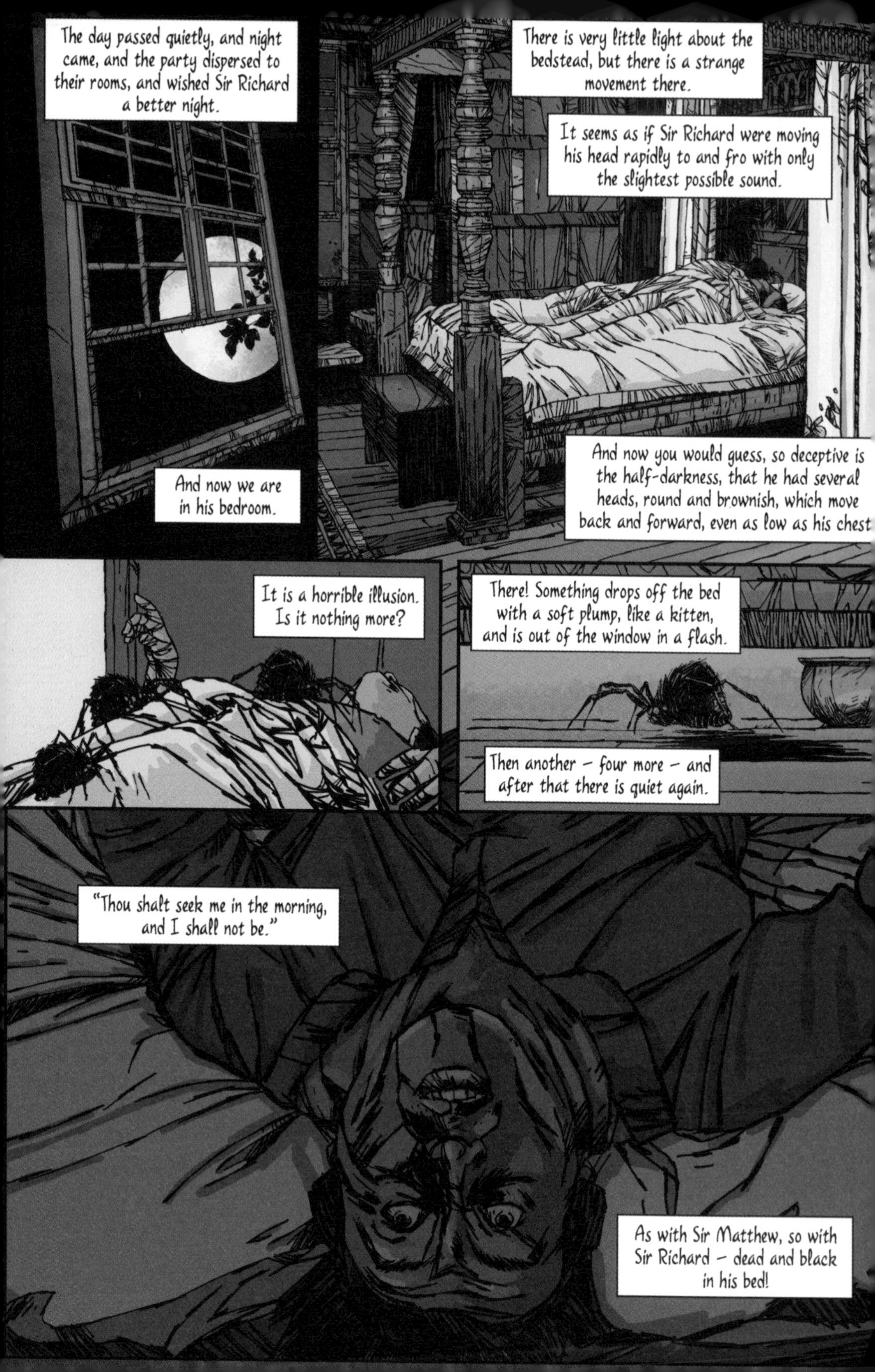
The day passed quietly, and night came, and the party dispersed to their rooms, and wished Sir Richard a better night.
And now we are in his bedroom.
There is very little light about the bedstead, but there is a strange movement there.
It seems as if Sir Richard were moving his head rapidly to and fro with only the slightest possible sound.
And now you would guess, so deceptive is the half-darkness, that he had several heads, round and brownish, which move back and forward, even as low as his chest
It is a horrible illusion. Is it nothing more?
There! Something drops off the bed with a soft plump, like a kitten, and is out of the window in a flash.
Then another – four more – and after that there is quiet again.
"Thou shalt seek me in the morning, and I shall not be."
As with Sir Matthew, so with Sir Richard – dead and black in his bed!

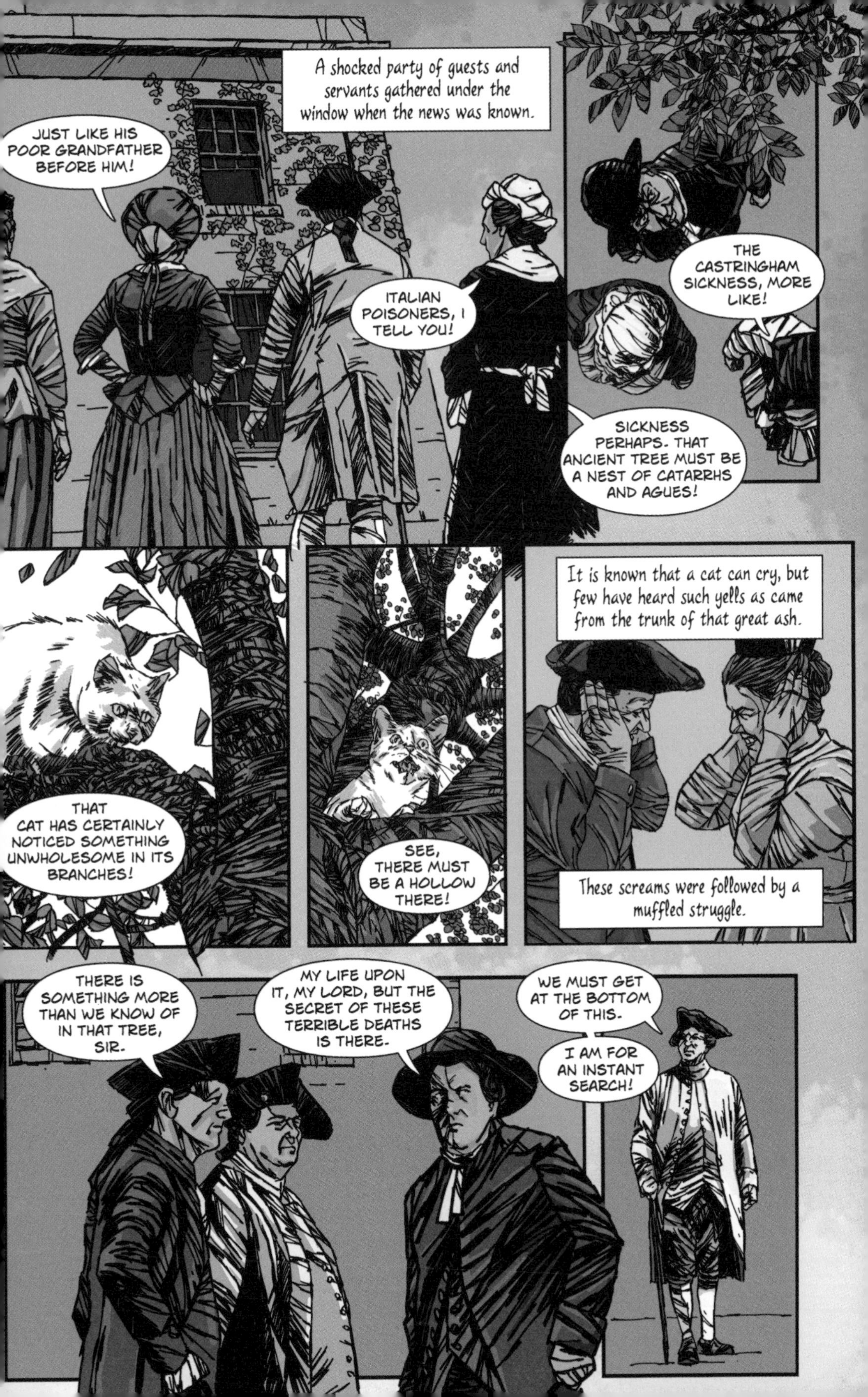
A shocked party of guests and servants gathered under the window when the news was known.
JUST LIKE HIS POOR GRANDFATHER BEFORE HIM!
ITALIAN POISONERS, I TELL YOU!
THE CASTRINGHAM SICKNESS, MORE LIKE!
SICKNESS PERHAPS. THAT ANCIENT TREE MUST BE A NEST OF CATARRHS AND AGUES!
THAT CAT HAS CERTAINLY NOTICED SOMETHING UNWHOLESOME IN ITS BRANCHES!
SEE, THERE MUST BE A HOLLOW THERE!
It is known that a cat can cry, but few have heard such yells as came from the trunk of that great ash.
These screams were followed by a muffled struggle.
THERE IS SOMETHING MORE THAN WE KNOW OF IN THAT TREE, SIR.
MY LIFE UPON IT, MY LORD, BUT THE SECRET OF THESE TERRIBLE DEATHS IS THERE.
WE MUST GET AT THE BOTTOM OF THIS.
I AM FOR AN INSTANT SEARCH!

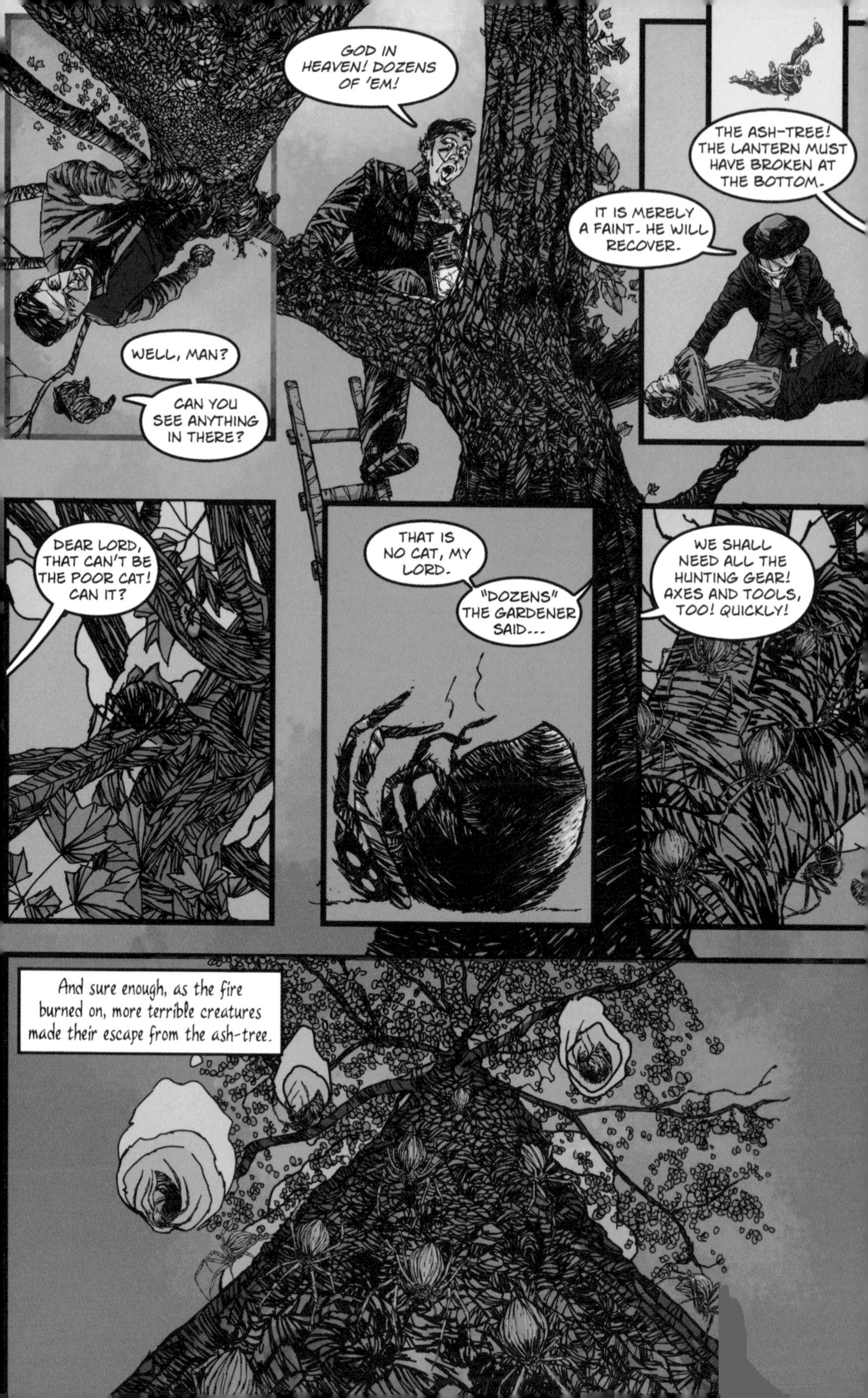
GOD IN HEAVEN! DOZENS OF 'EM!
WELL, MAN?
CAN YOU SEE ANYTHING IN THERE?
THE ASH-TREE! THE LANTERN MUST HAVE BROKEN AT THE BOTTOM.
IT IS MERELY A FAINT. HE WILL RECOVER.
DEAR LORD, THAT CAN'T BE THE POOR CAT! CAN IT?
THAT IS NO CAT, MY LORD.
"DOZENS" THE GARDENER SAID...
WE SHALL NEED ALL THE HUNTING GEAR! AXES AND TOOLS, TOO! QUICKLY!
And sure enough, as the fire burned on, more terrible creatures made their escape from the ash-tree.

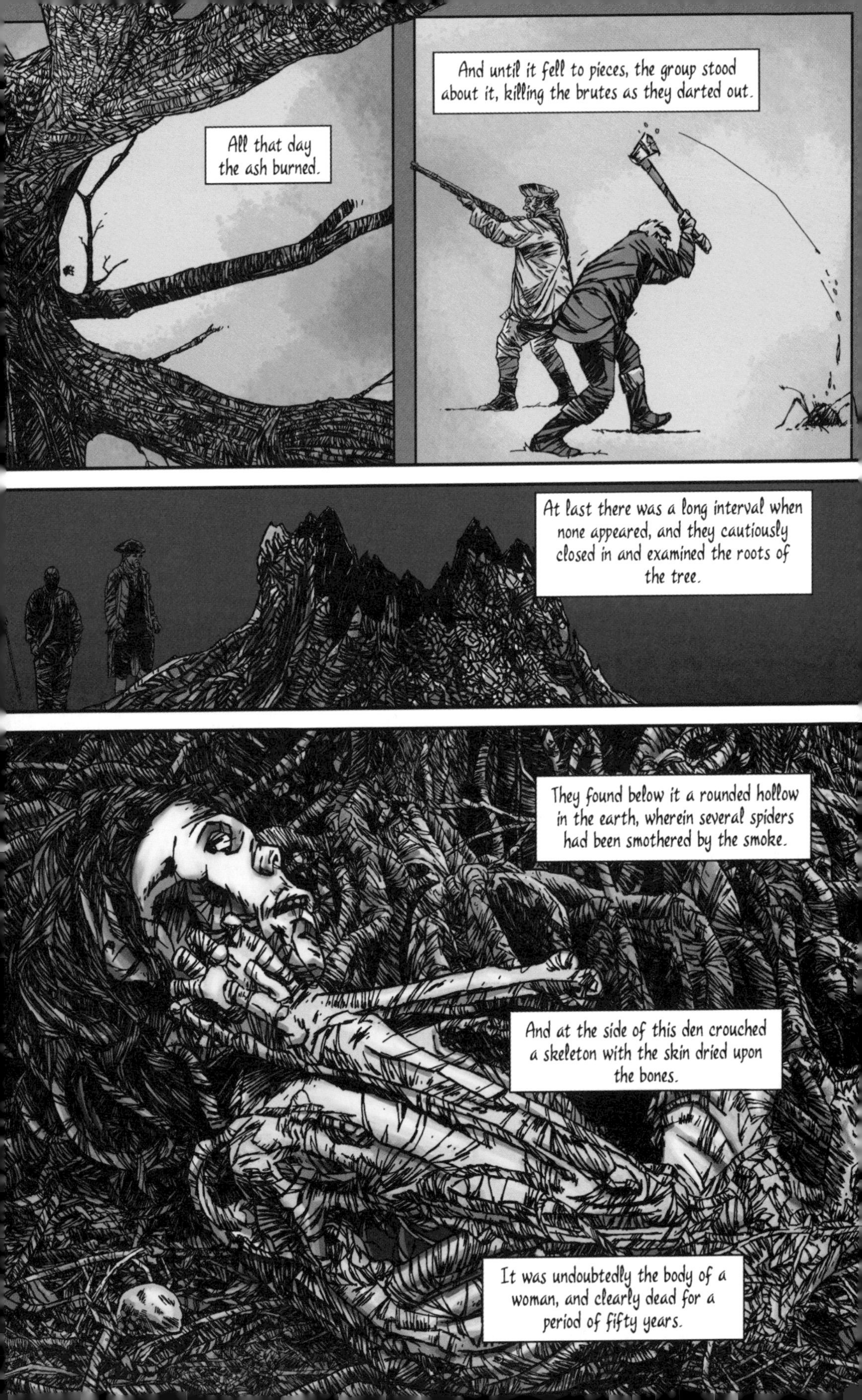
All that day the ash burned.
And until it fell to pieces, the group stood about it, killing the brutes as they darted out.
At last there was a long interval when none appeared, and they cautiously closed in and examined the roots of the tree.
They found below it a rounded hollow in the earth, wherein several spiders had been smothered by the smoke.
And at the side of this den crouched a skeleton with the skin dried upon the bones.
It was undoubtedly the body of a woman, and clearly dead for a period of fifty years.

ADAPTERS

LEAH MOORE AND JOHN REPPION

Husband and wife writing team Leah Moore and John Reppion have been working together since 2003. During their career, the duo have adapted works by Bram Stoker, H.P. Lovecraft and Lewis Carroll into comics, and have written original stories featuring such iconic characters as Sherlock Holmes, Doctor Who and Red Sonja.

ARTISTS

ANEKE

Aneke is an illustrator and animator from Madrid, with degrees in audiovisual communication and digital and visual art. Following her move into comics around five years ago, she has worked extensively for Dynamite on properties including *Damsels*, *Battlestar Galactica 1880*, *Red Sonja* and *Vampirella*. While striving to create good drawings and stories, she hopes to work on her own titles in the not-too-distant future.

KIT BUSS

Kit Buss is a London-based artist with a long-standing passion for comics and the macabre. Her previous works include Channel 4's *The Thrill Electric* and how-to-draw books for Barron's Educational Series, and she is currently an official artist for Geek and Sundry's D&D-based show *Critical Role*. She is eternally troubled by the irony of loving horror while being too afraid to watch it, leading to a complex relationship akin to that of a cat's with a fish tank.

FOUAD MEZHER

Based in Lebanon, Fouad Mezher works as an illustrator on a range of projects, with a primary focus on comics and children's books. Comics he has co-authored have appeared in *Samandal Comics Magazine*, *Risha Project* and *Irene*. They have featured deaths caused by pens, giant feet and an assortment of mutant animals.

ALISDAIR WOOD

Alisdair Wood is an illustrator and designer. Although primarily working in video games, including such franchises as *Grand Theft Auto*, *Red Dead Redemption* and *Max Payne*, he has also worked on other M.R. James projects with Ghosts & Scholars and A Podcast to the Curious. Currently he co-creates and draws for *Horrere*, an ongoing classic horror comic anthology. He lives and works in central Scotland.